REINCARNATION

THE BEST SHORT STORIES OF

R.B. CUNNINGHAME GRAHAM

D1592372

New Haven and New York

TICKNOR & FIELDS

1980

C. 2

Library of Congress Cataloging in Publication Data
Graham, Robert Bontine Cunninghame, 1852–1936.
  Reincarnation.

  First published in 1979 under title: Beattock for
Moffat and the best of R.B. Cunninghame Graham.
  CONTENTS: Reincarnation.—Mist in Monteith.—A
hegira. [etc.]
  I. Title.
PZ3.G7618Re   1980   [PR6013.R19]   823'.8   79–28208
ISBN 0–89919–004–9

Printed in the United States of America

V 10 9 8 7 6 5 4 3 2 1

CONTENTS

SOME NOTES ON R.B. CUNNINGHAME GRAHAM

(1852–1936)

by *ALANNA KNIGHT**

ROBERT BONTINE CUNNINGHAME GRAHAM, three parts Scots, one part Spanish, an aristocrat on all four sides and descended from the noblest blood in Scotland, was born in London. The fireworks just exploded outside No 5 Cadogan Square on May 24, 1852 were more appropriate to the birth of this future incendiary than in celebration of Queen Victoria's thirty-third birthday.

In Edinburgh, the last sedan chairs had just vanished from the streets. Sir Walter Scott had been dead for twenty years and Robert Louis Stevenson was eighteen months old, a sickly child, unlikely to survive. *The Scotsman* concerned itself with stamping out the slave trade in Africa and the plight of some four hundred destitute families from Skye seeking aid to emigrate to Australia. In Edinburgh's New Town, aristocratic old ladies were downright coarse in language and manners regarding the natural functions, behaviour which belonged to a more raffish age and which was, as yet, neither dimmed nor chastened by 'the young Hanoverian upstart' who occupied the English throne. Old gentlemen sipped their *usquebaugh* and sighed over fathers 'out' in the '45, little dreaming that Cunninghame Graham and patriots of that ilk would breathe new life into those old ghosts with the forming of the Scottish National Party in 1928 and the revolutionary concept of Home Rule for Scotland.

The eighty-four years of his life spanned a time of change greater than any before in the history of man. When he was three years old, the Crimean war was fought, in the traditional chessboard

* Alanna Knight is a Scottish writer of novels, short stories, and plays for stage, radio, and television.

4

style, with cavalry ranged on horses in brilliant uniforms and more obscure human lives for pawns. The bloody and terrible hand-to-hand fighting in the trenches of Flanders belonged to a century as yet unborn. When he died in 1936, the world was virtually on the threshold of space travel and in Spain there was Civil War, that grim dress rehearsal for World War II and the ultimate horror of Hiroshima. Passengers regularly crossed the Atlantic by aeroplane, business was conducted by disembodied voices over frail wires connecting the distant corners of the world and another magic flickering world, the cinema which had terrified its first audiences as the work of the devil, had already borne fruit in the shape of television.

Cunninghame Graham's childhood showed little evidence of the man who was to emerge, except for a hearty dislike of the English public school system. In common with may writers-in-embryo, he showed scant concern for the purely academic measure of success.

He came to authorship late, aged forty, at the end of a stormy political career lasting six years as Member of Parliament for North-West Lanarkshire. For the rest of his life he wrote prolifically—travel books, a biography of his colourful ancestor 'Doughty Deeds' Graham, eleven histories of Latin America and fourteen volumes of short stories and sketches.

His stories and sketches unconsciously portray a fighting man for whom attacking injustice was his *raison d'etre*. Sophistry he could not abide, but human failings, foibles and shortcomings fascinated him. The failings of the uneducated, unmoneyed underdog, he could accept. The same weaknesses exploited by the rich and powerful for the enjoyment of the rich and powerful, he could not.

A true romantic, he despised the smug hypocricies committed in the name of religion. 'There are only two classes', he declared, 'the genuine and the humbug.'

A founder of the Scottish Labour Party, friend of Keir Hardie and Scottish miners alike, he differed from his Socialist colleagues in that his written and verbal attacks on exploitations were not laced with the cliches, platitudes and slogan that summarised the working class of a century ago and still saddle the movement today. More Socialists than the radical reformers, John Burns and John Maclean, pilloried Cunninghame Graham as 'one of those damned aristos dabbling in Socialism'. Looking askance at his noble birth— this man Andrew Lang called 'the uncrowned king of Scots'—they were content to assure themselves that however well-meaning the Laird of Gartmore's sentiments, he would be no more in touch with the common man and revolution than "the pig-tailed pipe-clayed generals of the past, whose hearts," said Cunninghame Graham, "were not more hard than are the hearts of their tweed-clad descendants who nowadays blow you a thousand savages to paradise then sit down to lunch."

Of the two biographies written in 1932 and 1937, Herbert Faulkner West's *A Modern Conquistador* (Cranley & Day) was hampered by having its subject very much alive. Cunninghame Graham had still four more crowded years to live, while A.J. Tschiffely's *Don Roberto* (Heineman) also suffered necessary omissions dictated by discretion to friends still alive. Besides the natural affection and respect for a beloved friend of considerable charm, they treated him as a writer whose work mirrors his reputation. There is little evidence to support this, principally because he had established no respectable public reputation until 1905 by which time ten books had been published.

Respectable? Not according to Cunninghame Graham: "Nothing more false," he retorted. "For the most part all books are written from vanity, for hope of gain, either pecuniary or of some other nature, and now and then to please the writer, for it is known that that some have gone to sea for pleasure, and sailors say that those who do so would go to hell for fun."

Until 1895, when *Notes on the District of Mentieth* appeared, he had led a lively enough career. He had been imprisoned on three continents. At eighteen, by the revolutionary army in Argentina, when he was forced at knife-point to ride and fight with them; the second time in Morocco by the Kaid on his secret journey to the Forbidden City of Tarudant where no Christian had ever set foot, the third time for his part in the Battle of Trafalgar

Square, which began as a demonstration to petition for the release of the Irish patriot William O'Brien, and ended in political history as 'Bloody Sunday', November 13, 1887. But if the humour that remained with him during six weeks in Pentonville is any guide, he was no hangdog martyr taking a masochistic delight in being jailed. Asked how he found it later, he shrugged: "All right, but I wouldn't send my friends to it."

Why did the cause of the underdog—prostitutes, gauchos, Indians, horses—move him to passionate eloquence? What awakening of social conscience drove him to embrace the cause of Socialism in its pioneering days when it was neither popular nor fashionable?

Why did injustice to one man, Parnell, victimised because of the O'Shea scandal, drive Cunninghame Graham to the same anger as the plight of a whole race of men, the American Indians? At a time when adultery was no polite dinner-table topic, he had the temerity to blaze forth in the national press with a letter on Parnell which began: "Yes, I know. 'Thou shalt not commit adultery'. That is to say: 'Thou shalt not be found out committing adultery'. . ."

The Empire Builders to whom he prefaced *Mirages* (his last book written just before his death in 1936), must have felt the sun setting uncomfortably near when they read his three letters to the Press on American Indians which contained such comments as:

". . .when white troops, well-armed with all the newest murderous appliances of scientific warfare, shoot down men whose ignorance of their proper calling clearly proves them to be savages, the act is invariably spoken of as a 'glorious victory'. . .if the aforesaid braceless, breechless knaves, in precisely the same manner, shoot our 'glorious troops' their proceeding become a 'bloody massacre', a 'treacherous ambuscade' or something of a low-priced nature of that sort."

Doubtless Queen Victoria was not amused to have her statesmen dismissed as "political cheapjacks" and Britannia as "this jolly old roast-beef, plum pudding dunderheaded port-wine-and-Bible old country of ours." Even Mr. Gladstone was not safe from his acid wit: "I sometimes wish I could believe in religion," Cunninghame Graham declared, "for if I did I could be sure that Gladstone is in hell."

Shortly after he left the House of Commons in 1892, having "endured the concentrated idiocy of the Asylum for Incapables at Westminster for six years," he began writing in earnest. From then on he was increasingly accepted as a champion of injustice, the Radical Movement, Home Rule for Ireland and Scottish Independence.

His short stories are his personal memorial, just as poets survive in the main by their shorter works. But apart from an occasional anthologised or broadcast short story, his work has long been unpublished and the present anthology is long overdue. The last appeared in 1952. A master of the *genre*, he called it "the verbiage by which we put a fig leaf over the realities of life." Tender, ironic, they are written with wit and humour: "For wit," said he, "is but a varnish on the mind, a brightness and and exterior polish, bringing out, no doubt, the colour; but humour is the recompense which man made for himself after the Fall and when first sorrow came into the world."

If he has been temporarily lost to our generation, to whom the world before 1936 is history, he was greatly respected by the writers of his time. His vivid flamboyant personality, his sense of drama and love of an audience, his elegance and sweeping gestures, his superb voice, made Cunninghame Graham a man many might hate but few would ever forget, for despite the rapier sharp wit, his Quixotic nature contained genuine tenderness, compassion and mercy.

William Morris, H.G. Wells, Edward Garnett, T.E. Lawrence, H.M. Tomlinson, Sir William Rothenstein and the artists Sir Max Beerbohm, Sir John Lavery and J.A. MacNeil Whistler were among his many friends.

Frank Harris (Editor of the *Saturday Review*) remarked on Cunninghame Graham's account of William Morris's funeral: "An amateur genius; it's a pity he hasn't to earn a living by his pen" — to which sentiment George Bernard Shaw replied: "And a good thing for us; he'd wipe the floor with us all if he often wrote like that." Shaw, whose love of his fellow men was not his outstanding characteristic, admired Cunninghame Graham to the extent of using *Mogreb-El-Acksa* as his inspiration for *Captain Brassbound's Conversion* and immortalised his statement in the House of Commons: "I *never* withdraw" as the words of the hero of *Arms and the Man:* "I *never* apologise".

A precious few writers of our own time, the late Sir Compton Mackenzie, Hugh MacDiarmid and Wendy Wood, were still young enough in those sunset days at the end of his life to call Don Roberto 'friend'. His intimates were W.H. Hudson, Edward Garnett, Wilfred Scawen Blunt and Joseph Conrad (to whom he dedicated *Progress*, Conrad called him *The Prince of Preface-Writers* and a preface is the factor common to all his books of short stories. In *A Hatchment,* he describes it thus: "That on which the critics may take off the keen edge of their wit, just as in times gone by in low-class schools, they served the suet pudding out before the meat."

Many of his prefaces are, in fact, short stories in their own right, such as the Preface to *Charity,* which tells the story of a Spanish prostitute who falls in love with Scudamore, an English officer. The romance ends with Scudamore deserting her and saying to a shipboard acquaintance as the boat departs: "Good God, a pretty sight I should have looked travelling about, dragging a Spanish whore. . .I liked her well enough, but what I say is, Charity begins at home, my boy. Ah, there's the dinner bell!"

His stories run to no set pattern except when dealing with death, a subject, in Scotland, that vies only with ministers and graveyards as a topic of national humour. He cuts away the humour that for centuries the North Britons have used in time of stress to examine why a Scot thinks with his heart and not his head. His interest, like Goethe, lay more in probing the life of a community through the death of one of its members for "pre-occupation with immortality is for the upper classes, particularly ladies with nothing to do."

Not for Cunninghame Graham ''those long catalogues of quite unnecessary works of unknown and perhaps justly forgotten writers. . .which masquerade as prefaces like a misshapen maiden at a fancy dress ball who dressed up as Mary Queen of Scots. Your real and right preface should resemble Cervantes' introduction to his second part, in which he put his life's blood and his soul; or the last effort which he penned, his foot just resting in the stirrup (as he says) which none can read without a tightening of the heart. . . after these, what can your modern preface-monger do?''

One wonders what he would have written of our modern world. A born revolutionary, perhaps he would be airing his views in vitriol or turning the air blue at Trafalgar Square rallies and gleefully causing embarrassment to television interviewers on late night 'chat' programmes, passionately advocating lost causes, world peace or wild life preservation. For the questions he asked then are the questions of all time and these short stories provide, if not all the right answers, then at least some very spirited attempts.

''In the phantasmagoria we call the world, most things and men are ghosts,'' he wrote, ''or at the best but ghosts of ghosts, so vaporous and insubstantial that they scarcely cast a shadow on the grass. That which is most abiding with us is the recollection of the past. . .''

This past is vividly portrayed in this volume, his personal memorial. His epitaph on the Dumbarton Monument reads: "Famous Author Traveller and Horseman. Patriotic Scot and Citizen of the World. He was a Master of Life, a King Among Men.'' To these words might well have been added his own statement about the poet Wilfred Scawen Blunt: ''Born out of his generation, as are most of men who achieve anything but mere material success.''

REINCARNATION

ISBILIEH, as the Moors called Seville, had never looked more Moorish than on that day in spring. The scent of azahar hung in the air; from patio and from balcony floated the perfume of albahaca and almoraduz, plants brought to Seville by the Moors from Nabothea and from Irak-el-Hind. The city of the royal line of the Beni-Abbad was as if filled with a reminiscence of its past of sensuality and blood. The mountains of the Axarafe loomed in a violet haze, and seemed so near, you felt that you could touch them with your hand. The far-off sierras above Ronda looked jagged, and as if fortified to serve as ramparts against the invasion of the African from his corresponding sierra in the country of the Angera, across the narrow straits. Over the Giralda came the faint, pink tinge which evening imparts, in Seville, to all the still remaining Moorish work, making the finest specimen of the architecture of the Moors in Spain look as delicate and new as when the builder, he who built at Marákesh and Rabat two other towers of similar design, raised it in honour of the one God, and the great camel-driver who stands beside his throne. Down the great river for which the Christians never found a better name than that left by the Moorish dogs, the yellow tide ran lazily, swaying alike the feluccas with their tall, tapering yards, the white Norwegian fruit schooners, and the sea coffins from the port of London, tramps out of Glasgow, and the steam colliers from the Hartlepools or Newcastle-on-Tyne. The great cathedral in which lies Ferdinand Columbus, the most southern Gothic building in all Europe, built on the site of the chief mosque said to have been as large as that of Córdoba, rose from the Court of Oranges, silent as a vast tomb, and seemed protected from the town by its raised walk, fenced in with marble pillars and massive iron chains. The Alcázar, and The Tower of Gold, the churches, especially St. John's Beside the Palm, seemed to regret their builders, as, I think, do all the Saracenic buildings throughout Spain. Though ignorant of all the plastic arts, taking their architecture chiefly from the two forms of tent and palm tree, their literature so conceived as to be almost incomprehensible to the peoples of the north, the tribes who came from the Hedjaz, the Yemen, and beyond Hadramut have left their imprint on whatever land they passed. They comprehended that life is first, the chiefest business which man has to do, and so subordinated to it all the rest. Their eyes, their feet, their verse, and their material-istic view of everything have proved indelible wherever they have camped. They and their horses have stamped themselves for ever on the world. Even to-day, their speech remains embedded, like a mosaic, in the vocabulary of Southern Spain, giving the language strength.

Notable things have passed in Seville since Ojeda, before he sailed for the new-found Indies, ran along the beam fixed at a giddy height in the Giralda and threw a tennis-ball over the weather-vane to show the Catholic kings and the assem-bled crowd the firmness of his head. Since San Fernando drove out the royal house of the Beni-Abbad, and Motamid, the poet king, took sanctuary in Mequinez, as Abd-el-Wahed notes in his veracious history of the times, much has occurred and has been chronicled in blood. In the Alcázar, Pedro el Justiciero loved Maria de Padilla; in it he had made the fish-pond where the degenerate Charles the Second sat a-fishing, whilst his empire slipped out of his hands. The Caloró from Hind, Multán, or from whatever trans-Caucasian or cis-Himalayan province they set out from, ages ago, had come, and spreading over Spain, fixed themselves firmly in the part of Seville called the Triana, after the Emperor Trajan who was born there, as some say, and where to-day they chatter Romany, traffic in horses, tell fortunes, and behave as if the world were a great oyster which they could open with their tongues, so wheedling and well hung.

So, on the evening of which I write, a Sunday in the month of May, the bull-fight was just over, leaving behind it that mixed air of sensuousness and blood which seems to hover over Seville after each show of bulls, as it may once have hovered, after a show of gladiators, about Italica in the old Roman days.

The fight was done, and all the tourists, after condemning Spanish barbarism, had taken boxes to a man, and come away delighted with the picturesqueness of the show.

Trumpets had sounded, and the horses, all of which had done more service to mankind than any fifty men, and each of whom had as much right, by every law of logic and anatomy, to have a soul, if souls exist, as had the wisest of philosophers, had suffered martyrdom. Hungry and ragged, they had trodden on their entrails, received their wounds without a groan, without a tear, without a murmur, faithful to the end; had borne their riders out of danger, fallen upon the bloody sand at last with quivering tails, and, biting their poor, parched and bleeding tongues, had died just as the martyrs died at Lyons or in Rome, as dumb and brave as they.

In the arena the light-limbed men, snake-like and glittering in their tinselly clothes, had capered nimbly before the bull, placing their banderillas deftly on his neck.

Waiting until he almost touched them, they placed one foot upon his forehead, and stepping lightly across the horns, had executed what is called "el salto de trascuerno." Then leaping with a pole, they had alighted on the other side of him like thistledown, had dived behind the screen, had caught and held the furious beast an instant by the tail, and after having played a thousand antics, running the gamut, known to the intelligent as "volapié," "galleo," "tijerilla," "verónica," and "chatré," escaped as usual with their lives.

The espada had come forward, mumbled his "boniment" in Andaluz, swung his montera round his shoulder towards the presidential throne, and after sticking his sword, first in the muscles of the neck, from which it sprang into the air, and fell, bloody and twisted, on the sand, taking another from an attendant sprite, butchered his bull at last, amid thunders of applause.

Blood on the sand; the sun reflected back like flame from the white walls; upon the women's faces cascarilla; a fluttering of red and yellow fans; lace veils on glossy hair, looking like new-fallen snow on a black horse's back, all made a picture of the meeting of the east and west to which the water-sellers' voices added, as they called "Agua," in a voice so guttural, it sounded like the screaming of a jay.

A scent of blood and sweat rose from the plaza, and acted like an aphrodisiac on the crowd.

Bold-looking women squeezed each other's hands, and looked ambiguously at one another, as if they were half men. Youths with their hair cut low upon their foreheads, loose, swinging hips, and eyes that met the glance as if they were half girls, pressed one against the other on the seats. Blood, harlotry, sun, gay flowers, and waving palm trees, women with roses stuck behind their ears, mules covered up in harness of red worsted, cigar girls, gipsies, tourists, soldiers and the little villainous-looking urchins, who, though born old, do duty in the south as children, formed a kaleidoscope. The plaza vomited out the crowd, just as the Roman amphitheatre through its vomitorium expelled its crowd of blood-delighting Roman citizens, "Civis Romanus sum," and all the rest of it.

The stiff, dead horses, all were piled into a cart, their legs sticking out, pathetic and grotesque, between the bars. A cart of sand was emptied on the blood, which lay in blackening pools here and there in the plaza, and then the espada, smoking a cigar, emerged like Agag, delicately, and drove off, the focus of all eyes. Girls swarmed in the streets, sailing along with their incomparable walk unrivalled in the world, and in the Calle de la Pasión the women of the life stood against open, but barred windows, painted and powdered, and with an eye to business as they scanned passing men.

Lovers stood talking from the streets by signs to girls upon the balcony, their mother's presence hidden behind the curtain in the dark, and the space intervening, keeping their virtue safe.

Sometimes a man leaned up against the grating and whispered to his sweetheart through the bars, holding her hand in his. The passers-by affected not to see them, and either stepped into the street or looked with half-averted eyes at the first act in life's great comedy.

In the great palm-tree planted square the salmon-coloured plaster seats were filled with men, who seemed to live there day and night, contributing their quota to the ceaseless national expenditure of talk. On this occasion they discussed, being all "inteligentes," each incident and action of the fight, the old men deprecating modern innovation and sighing for the times and styles of Cucháres, or el Zeño Romero, he who first brought the art of bull-fighting from heaven, as his admirers say. If a girl, rich or poor, a countess from Madrid, or maiden of the Caloró from the Triana, chanced to pass, they criticized her, as a prospective buyer does a horse or as a dealer looks down a slave at Fez. Her eyes, her feet, her air, each detail of her dress, were all passed in review, and if found pleasing, then came the approving, "Blessed be your mother!" with other compliments of a nature to make a singer at a Paris café-concert blush. The recipient took it all as a matter of everyday occurrence, and with a smile or word of thanks, according to her rank, pursued the uneven tenor of her way with heightened colour, and perhaps a little more "meneo" of her hips and swaying of her breasts.

In the Calle Sierpes, the main artery and chief bazaar, roofed with an awning right from end to end, the people swarmed like ants, passing, and then repassing in a stream. Cafés were gorged with clients, all talking of the bull-fight, cursing the Government, or else disputing of the beauty and the nature of the women of their respective towns. The clubs, with windows of plate glass down to the ground, showed the "haute gomme" lounging in luxury upon their plush-upholstered chairs, stiff in their English clothes, and sweating blood and water in the attempt to look like Englishmen, and to keep up an unconcerned appearance under the public gaze. Girls selling lemonade, horchata, agraz, with the thick, sticky sweetmeats, and the white, flaky pastry flavoured with fennel and angelica, left by the Moors in Spain, went up and down crying their wares, and offering themselves to anyone who wished to venture half a dollar on the chance. The shops were full of all those unconsidered trifles, which in Spain alone can find a market, cheap and abominably nasty, making one think that our manufactories must be kept running with a view to furnish idiots or blind men with things they do not want.

After the gospel comes the sermon; sherry after soup, and when the bloodshed of the day has stirred men's pulses, they drift instinctively towards the dancing-houses, just as a drunkard in the morning turns back again to drink, to give another fillip to the blood. Men streamed to the Burrero, at whose narrow doors sat ancient hags selling stale flowers and cheaply painted match-boxes, pushing and striving in the narrow passage to make their way inside. The temple of the dance was an enormous building, barn-like and dusty, and with its emptiness made manifest by oil-lamps stuck about the walls.

The floor was sanded and in the middle of it, at little wooden tables, seated on rickety cane chairs, was the fine flower of the rascality of Spain, whilst round the walls stood groups of men, who by their dress might have been Chulos or Chalanes, loafers or horse-copers, all with their hair brushed forward on their foreheads and plastered to the head.

All wore tight trousers moulded to the hips, short and

frogged jackets, and all had flat felt hats with a stiff brim, which now and then they ran their fingers round to see if it was straight.

Others were wrapped in tattered cloaks, and mixed with them were herdsmen and some shepherds, with here and there a bull-fighter and here and there a pimp.

In the crank, shaky gallery was a dark box or two, unswept and quite unfurnished, save for a bunch or two of flowers painted upon the plaster, and a poor lithograph of the reigning sovereign, flanking a bull-fighter. One was quite empty, and in the other sat two foreign ladies, come to see life in Seville, who coughed and rubbed their eyes in the blue haze of cigarette smoke, which filled the building, just as the incense purifies a church with its mysterious fumes.

Set in a row across the stage, like flowers in a bed, were six or seven girls. Their faces painted in the fashion of the place, without concealment, just like the ladies whom Velázquez drew, gave them a look of artificiality, which their cheap boots, all trodden down at the heel, and hair dressed high upon the head, with a comb upon the top and a red flower stuck behind the ear, did little to redeem.

Smoking and pinching one another they sat waiting for their turn, exchanging jokes occasionally with their acquaintances in front, and now and then one or the other of them rising from her chair walked to the looking-glasses placed on each side of the stage, and put her hair in order, patting it gently at the side and shaking out her clothes, just as a bird shakes out its feathers after it rolls itself in dust.

On one side of the stage sat the musicians, two at the guitar and two playing small instruments known as "bandurrias"—a cross between the mandolin and a guitar, played with a piece of quill. The women suddenly began to clap their hands in a strange rhythm, monotonous at first, but which at length, like the beating of a tom-tom, makes the blood boil, quiets the audience, stills conversation, and focusses all eyes upon the stage. The strange accompaniment, with the hands swept across the strings, making a whir as when a turkey drags its wings upon the ground, went on eternally. Then one broke out into a half-wild song, the interval so strange, the time so wavering, and so mixed up the rhythm, that at first hearing it scarcely seems more pleasing than the howling of a wolf, but bit by bit goes to the soul, stirs up the middle marrow of the bones, and leaves all other music ever afterwards tame and unpalatable.

The singing terminated abruptly, as it seemed, for no set reason, and died away in a prolonged high note, and then a girl stood up, encouraged by her fellows with shouts of "Venga Juana," "Vaya salerosa," and a cross-fire of hats thrown on the stage, and interjections from the audience of "Tu sangre" or "Tu enerpo" and the inspiriting clap of hands, which never ceases till the dancer, exhausted, sinks down upon a chair. Amongst the audience, drinking their manzanilla in little tumblers about the thickness of a piece of sugar-cane, eating their boquerones, ground nuts, and salted olives, the fire of criticism never stopped, as everyone in Seville of the lower classes is a keen critic both of dancing-girls and bulls. Of the elder men, a gipsy, though shouting "Salero!" in a perfunctory manner, seemed discontented, and recalled the prowess of a dancer long since dead, by name Aurora, surnamed La Cujiñi, and gave it as his faith that since her time no girl had ever mastered all the mysteries of the dance. The Caloró, who always muster strong at the Burrero, all were upon his side, and seemed inclined to enforce their arguments with their shears, which, as most of them maintain themselves by clipping mules, they carry in their sash.

Then, just as the discussion seemed about to end in a free fight, a girl stepped out to dance. None had remarked her sitting quietly beside the rest; still, she was slightly different in appearance from all the others in the room, both in her air and dress.

A gipsy at first sight, with the full lustrous eyes her people brought from far Multán, dressed in a somewhat older fashion than the rest, her hair brought low upon her forehead and hanging on her shoulders after the style of 1840, her skirt much flounced, low shoes tied round the ankle, a Chinese shawl across her shoulders, and with a look about her, as she walked to the middle of the stage, as of a mare about to kick. A whisper to the first guitar caused him with a smile to break into a tango, his instrument well "requintado," striking the chords with every finger of his hand at the same instant, as the wild Moorish melody jingled and jarred out and quivered in the air.

She stood a moment motionless, her eyes distending slowly and focussing the attention of the audience on her, and then a sort of shiver seemed to run over her, the feet gently began to scrape along the floor, her naked arms moved slowly with her fingers curiously bent, and meant perhaps to indicate by their position the symbols of the oldest of religions, and, as the gipsies say, she drew the heart of every onlooker into her net of love. Twisting her hips till they seemed ready to disjoint, and writhing like a snake, dragging her skirt up on the stage, she drew herself up to her full height, thrust all her body forward, her hands moved faster, and the short sleeves slipped back exhibiting black tufts of hair under her arms, glued to her skin with sweat. Then she wreathed forwards, backwards, looked at the audience with defiance, took a man's hat from off the stage, placed it upon her head, put both her arms akimbo, swayed to and fro, but still kept writhing as if her veins were full of quicksilver. Little by little the frenzy died away, her eyes grew dimmer, the movements of the body slower, then with a final stamp, and a hoarse guttural cry, she stood a moment quiet, as it is called, "dormida," that is, asleep, looking a very statue of impudicity and lust. The audience sat a moment spellbound, with open mouths like satyrs, and in the box where were the foreign ladies, one had turned pale resting her head upon the other's shoulder, who held her round the waist. Then with a mighty shout, the applause broke forth, hats rained upon the stage, "Oles" and "Vayas" rent the air, and the old gipsy bounded on the table with a shout, "One God, one Cujiñi"; but in the tumult, La Cujiñi had disappeared, gone from the eyes of Caloró and of Busné, Gipsy and Gentile, and the Burrero never saw her more.

Perhaps at witches' sabbaths she still dances, or perhaps in that strange Limbo where the souls of gipsies and their donkeys dree their weird, she writhes and dislocates her hips in the Romalis, or in the Ole, she drags her skirts on the floor, with a faint rustling sound.

Sometimes the curious may see her still, dancing before a Venta in the blurred outline of a Spanish lithograph, her head thrown back, her hair "en catagón," with one foot pointing to a hat to show her power over, and her contempt for, all the sons of man, just as she did upon that evening when she took a brief and fleeting reincarnation to breathe once more the air of Seville, heavy with perfume of spring flowers, mixed with the scent of blood.

MIST IN MENTEITH

SOME say the name Menteith meant a peat moss in Gaelic, and certainly peat mosses fill a third of the whole vale. However that may be, its chiefest attribute is mist. Shadows in summer play on the faces of the hills, and snow in winter spreads a cold carpet over the brown moss; but the mist stays the longest with us, and under it the semi-Highland, semi-Lowland valley puts on its most familiar air.

When billowing waves wreathe round the hills, and by degrees encroach upon the low, flat moors, they shroud the district from the world, as if they wished to keep it from all prying eyes, safe and inviolate. Summer and spring and winter all have their charms, either when the faint green of the baulked vegetation of the north breaks out, tender yet vivid, or when the bees buzz in the heather in the long days of the short, nightless summer, or when the streams run noiselessly under their shroud of ice in a hard frost. The autumn brings the rain, soaking and blurring everything. Leaves blotch and blacken, then fall swirling down on to the sodden earth.

On trees and stones, from fences, from the feals upon the tops of dykes, a beady moisture oozes, making them look as if they had been frosted. When all is ready for them, the mists sweep down and cover everything; from the interior of the darkness comes the cries of wild ducks, of herons as they sit upon the trees, and of geese passing overhead. Inside the wreaths of mist another world seems to have come into existence, something distinct from and antagonistic to mankind. When the mist once descends, blotting out the familiar features of the landscape, leaving perhaps the Rock of Stirling floating in the air, the three black trees upon the bare rock of the Fairy Hill growing from nothing, or the peak of the Cobbler, seeming to peer above enormous mountain ranges, though in reality nothing more vast than the long shoulder of Ben Lomond intervenes, the change has come that gives Menteith its special character.

There are mists all the world over, and in Scotland in particular; mists circling round the Western Islands, filling the glens and boiling in the corries of the hills mists that creep out to sea or in towards the land from seawards, threatening and dreadful-looking; but none like ours, so impalpable and strange, and yet so fitting to our low, flat mosses with our encircling hills. In older days they sheltered the marauders from the north, who in their gloom fell on the valley as if they had sprung from the night, plundered and burned and harried, and then retreated under cover of the mist, back to their fastnesses.

As they came through the Glen of Glenny, or the old road behind Ben Dhu, which comes out just a little east of Inver-trossachs, when the wind blew aside the sheltering wreaths of steam, and the rare gleams of sun fell on the shaggy band, striking upon the heads of their Lochaber axes, and again shifted and covered them from sight, they must have seemed a phantom army, seen in a dream, just between consciousness and sleep.

The lake, with its three islands, its giant chestnuts, now stag-headed and about to fall, the mouldering priory, the long church with its built-up, five-light window, the castle, overgrown with brushwood, and with a tree springing up from the middle hall, the heronry the rope of sand the fairies twisted, which would have made a causeway to the island had they not stopped just in the nick of time, the single tree that marks the gallows, and the old churchyard of the Port, all these the mist invests with a peculiar charm that they lack when the sun shines and shows them merely mouldering ruins and decaying trees.

So of the Flanders Moss. It, too, in mist seems to roll on for miles; its healthy surface turns to long waves that play against the foot of the low range of hills, and beat upon

Craigforth as if it were an island in the sea. Through wreaths of steam, the sullen Forth winds in and out between the peat hags, and when a slant of wind leaves it clear for an instant it looks mysterious and dark, as might a stream of quick-silver running down from a mine. When a fish leaps, the sound re-echoes like a bell, as it falls back into the water, and rings spread out till they are lost beneath the banks.

After a day or two of gloom life begins somehow or another to be charged with mystery; and, walking through the woods, instinctively you look about half in alarm as a roe bounds away, or from a fir-tree a capercailizie drums or flies off with a noise as if a moose was bursting through the trees.

Peat-smoke floats through the air from cottages a mile away, acrid and penetrating, and fills the nostrils with its scent. The little streams run with a muffled tinkle as if they wished to hide away from sight; rank, yellow ragweeds on their banks, bowed down with the thick moisture, all hang their heads as if they mourned for the lost sunshine and the day. Now and then leaves flutter down slowly to the ground like dying butterflies. Over the whole earth hangs, as it were, a sounding-board, intensifying everything, making the senses more acute, and carrying voices from a distance, focussed to the ear.

So through our mists a shepherd's dog barking a mile off, is heard as loudly as if it were a yard or two away, although the sound comes slowly to the hearing, as when old-fashioned guns hung fire and the report appeared to reach one through a veil. Thus does the past, with its wild legends, the raiders from the north, the Broken Men, the Saxon's Leap, the battles of the Grahams and the McGregors, come down to us veiled by the mist of time. In the lone churchyards, whose grass is always damp the whole year round, whose earth, when a new grave is dug, is always wet, so wet that not a stone rolls from it to the grass; the tombstones, with the lettering overgrown with lichens, only preserve the names of the old enemies who now lie side by side, in a faint shadowy way. The sword that marks the resting-place of the men of the most turbulent of all the races of that borderland is usually only the shadow of a sword, so well the mist has done its work, rounding off edges and obliterating chisel marks.

Boats on the Loch o' the Port, with oars muffled by the cloud of vapour that broods upon the lake, glide in and out of the thick curtain spread between the earth and sky, the figure of the standing fisher in the stern looming gigantic as he wields his rod in vain; for, in the calm, even the water-spiders leave a ripple as they run. In the low, mossy "parks" that lose themselves in beds of bulrushes before they join the lake, the Highland cattle stand at gaze, the damp congealing on their coats in whitish beadlets, and horses hang their heads disconsolately, for no matter in what climate they are born, horses are creatures of the sun. Under the shroud of gloom it seems that something strange is going on, something impalpable that gives the valley of Menteith its own peculiar air of sadness, as if no summer sun, no winter frost, no fierce March winds, or the chill cold of April, could ever really dry the tears of moisture that it lays up under the autumn mist. So all our walls are decked with a thick coating of grey lichen on the weather side that looks like flakes of leather, and on the lee side with a covering of bright, green moss.

Thatch moulders, and from it springs a growth of vegetation; a perpetual dripping from the eaves opens a little rill below it, in which the pebbles glisten as in a mountain stream.

Along the roads the scanty traffic rumbles fitfully, and on the Sabbath, down the steep path towards the little church, knots of fantastic figures seem to stalk like threatening phantoms. When they draw near, one sees that they were but the familiar faces of McKerrochar of Cullamoon, Graham of Tombreak, Campbell of Rinaclach, and Finaly Mitchell, dressed in their Sunday clothes. They pass the time of day, daunder a little in the damp kirkyard, so heaped with graves they have to pick their way between them just as sheep pick their way and follow one another on a steep mountain path, or when they cross a burn.

Although their talk runs on their daily life—the price of beasts at the last market or the tryst, upon bad seasons and the crops, all in the compassed and depreciatory vein characteristic of their calling and their race, they once have been fantastic figures towering above the dry-stone dykes that edge the road. That glory nothing can take away from them, or from the valley where they dwell.

Nothing is stable. Snows melt and rain gives place to sun, and sun to rain again; spring melts into summer, then autumn blends insensibly with winter, and the year is out. Men come and go, the Saxon speech replaces Gaelic; even traditions insensibly are lost.

The trees decay and fall, then they lie prone like the great hollow chestnut trunks, blackened by tourists' fires, in Inchmahome. Our hills and valleys all have changed their shapes under the action either of fire or ice. Life, faiths, ideals, all have changed. The Flanders Moss that was a sea is now crossed by a railway and by innumerable roads. What, then, shall we who have seen mists rising up all our lives, feared them as children, loved them in riper years, cling to, but mist?

Refuge of our wild ancestors, moulder of character, inspirer of the love of mystery, chief characteristic of the Keltic mind, spirit that watches over hills and valleys, lochs, clachans, bealachs and shaggy baadans, essence compounded of the water of the sky and earth, impalpable, dark and threatening, Fingal and Bran and Ossian, and he who in outstretching Ardnamurchan strung his harp to bless the birlinn of Clanranald, all have disappeared in thy grey folds.

Whether thou art death stealing amongst us, veiled, or life concealed behind a curtain, or but an emanation from the ground, which the poor student, studying in Aberdeen, working by day upon the wharves and poring over books at night, can explain as easily as he can solve all other mysteries, with his science primer, who shall say?

All that I know is that when the mantle of the damp rolls down upon us, battling with the rough oak copse upon Ben Dearch or Craigmore till all is swallowed up and a smooth surface stretches out over what, but half an hour before, was a thick wood of gnarled and secular trees that stood like piles stand up in an embankment, eaten by the sea, the mist has conquered.

Somehow, I think, its victory brings a sense of rest.

A HEGIRA

THE giant cypresses, tall even in the time of Montezuma, the castle of Chapultepec upon its rock (an island in the plain of Mexico), the panorama of the great city backed by the mountain range; the two volcanoes, the Popocatepetl and the Istacihuatl, and the lakes; the tigers in their cages, did not interest me so much as a small courtyard, in which, ironed and guarded, a band of Indians of the Apache tribe were kept confined. Six warriors, a woman and a boy, captured close to Chihuahua, and sent to Mexico, the Lord knows why; for generally an Apache captured was shot at once, following the frontier rule, which without difference of race was held on both sides of the Rio Grande, that a good Indian must needs be dead.

Silent and stoical the warriors sat, not speaking once in a whole day, communicating but by signs; naked except the breech-clout; their eyes apparently opaque, and looking at you without sight, but seeing everything; and their demeanour less reassuring than that of the tigers in the cage hard by. All could speak Spanish if they liked, some a word or two of English, but no one heard them say a word in either tongue. I asked the nearest if he was a Mescalero, and received the answer, "Mescalero-hay," and for a moment a gleam shone through their eyes, but vanished instantly, as when the light dies out of the wire in an electric lamp. The soldier at the gate said they were "brutes"; all sons of dogs, infidels, and that for his part he could not see why the "Gobierno" went to the expense of keeping them alive. He thought they had no sense; but in that showed his own folly, and acted after the manner of the half-educated man the whole world over, who knowing he can read and write thinks that the savage who cannot do so is but a fool; being unaware that, in the great book known as the world, the savage often is the better scholar of the two.

But five-and-twenty years ago the Apache nation, split into its chief divisions of Mescaleros, Jicarillas, Coyoteros, and Lipanes, kept a great belt of territory almost five hundred miles in length, and of about thirty miles in breadth, extending from the bend of the Rio Gila to El Paso, in a perpetual war. On both sides of the Rio Grande no man was safe; farms were deserted, cattle carried off, villages built by the Spaniards, and with substantial brick-built churches, mouldered into decay; mines were unworkable, and horses left untended for a moment were driven off in open day; so bold the thieves, that at one time they had a settled month for plundering, which they called openly the Moon of the Mexicans, though they did not on that account suspend their operations at other seasons of the year. Cochise and Mangas-Coloradas, Naked Horse, Cuchillo Negro, and others of their chiefs, were once far better known upon the frontiers than the chief senators of the congresses of either of the two republics; and in some instances these chiefs showed an intelligence, knowledge of men and things, which in another sphere would certainly have raised them high in the estimation of mankind.

The Shis-Inday (the people of the woods), their guttural language, with its curious monosyllable "hay" which they tacked on to everything, as "oro-hay" and "plata-hay"; their strange democracy, each man being chief of himself, and owing no allegiance to anyone upon the earth; all now have passed away, destroyed and swallowed up by the "Inday pindah lichoyi" (the men of the white eyes), as they used to call the Americans and all those northerners who ventured into their territory to look for "yellow iron." I saw no more of the Apaches, and, except once, never again met any one of them; but as I left the place the thought came to my mind: if any of them succeed in getting out, I am certain that the six or seven hundred miles between them and their country will be as nothing to them, and that their journey thither will be marked with blood. At Huehuetoca I joined the mule-train, doing the twenty miles which in those days was all the extent of railway in the country to the north, and lost my pistol in a crowd just as I stepped into the train, some "lepero" having abstracted it out of my belt when I was occupied in helping five strong men to get my horse into a cattle-truck. From Huehuetoca we marched to Tula, and there camped for the night, sleeping in a "mesón," built like an Eastern fondak round a court, and with a well for watering the beasts in the centre of the yard. I strolled about the curious town, in times gone by the Aztec capital, looked at the churches, built like fortresses, and coming back to the mesón before I entered the cell-like room without a window, and with a plaster bench on which to spread one's saddle and one's rugs, I stopped to talk with a knot of travellers feeding their animals on barley and chopped straw, grouped round a fire, and the whole scene lit up and rendered Rembrandtesque by the fierce glow of an ocote torch. So talking of the Alps and Apennines, or, more correctly, speaking of the Sierra Madre, and the mysterious region known as the Bolson de Mapimi, a district in those days as little known as is the Sus to-day, a traveller drew near. Checking his horse close by the fire, and getting off it gingerly, for it was almost wild, holding the hair mecate in his hand, he squatted down, the horse snorting and hanging back and setting rifle and machete jingling upon the saddle, he began to talk.

"Ave María purísima, had we heard the news?" What! a new revolution? Had Lerdo de Tejada reappeared again? or had Cortinas made another raid on Brownsbille? the Indios Bravos harried Chihuahua? or had the silver "conduct" coming from the mines been robbed? "Nothing of this, but a voice ran (corría una voz) that the Apache infidels confined in the courtyard of the castle of Chapultepec had broken loose. Eight of them, six warriors, a woman and a boy, had slipped their fetters, murdered two of the guard, and were supposed to be somewhere not far from Tula, and," as he thought, "making for the Bolson de Mapimi, the deserts of the Rio Gila, or the recesses of the mountains of the Santa Rosa range."

Needless to say, this put all in the mesón almost beside themselves; for the terror that the Indians inspired was at that time so real, that had the eight forlorn and helpless infidels appeared I verily believe they would have killed us all. Not that we were not brave, well armed—in fact, all loaded down with arms, carrying rifles and pistols, swords stuck between our saddle-girths, and generally so fortified as to resemble walking arsenals. But valour is a thing of pure convention, and these men who would have fought like lions against marauders of their own race, scarce slept that night for thinking on the dangers which they ran by the reported presence of those six naked men. The night passed by without alarm, as was to be expected, seeing that the court-yard wall of the mesón was at least ten feet high, and the gate solid ahuehuete clamped with iron, and padlocked like a gaol. At the first dawn, or rather at the first false dawn, when the fallacious streaks of pink flash in the sky and fade again to night, all were afoot. Horsemen rode out, sitting erect in their peaked saddles, toes stuck out and thrust into their curiously stamped toe-leathers; their chaparreras giving to their legs a look of being cased in armour, their poblano hats, with bands of silver or of tinsel, balanced like haloes on their heads.

Long trains of donkeys, driven by Indians dressed in leather, and bareheaded, after the fashion of their ancestors, crawled through the gate laden with pulque, and now and then a single Indian followed by his wife set off on foot, carrying a crate of earthenware by a broad strap depending from his head. Our caravan, consisting of six two-wheeled mule-carts, drawn by a team of six or sometimes eight gaily harnessed mules, and covered with a tilt made from the istle,

creaked through the gate. The great mesón remained
deserted, and by degrees, as a ship leaves the coast, we struck
into the wild and stony desert country, which, covered with
a whitish dust of alkali, makes Tula an oasis; then the great
church sank low, and the tall palm trees seemed to grow
shorter; lastly church, palms and towers, and the green fields
planted with aloes, blended together and sank out of sight,
a faint white misty spot marking their whereabouts, till at
last it too faded and melted into the level plain.

Travellers in a perpetual stream we met journeying to
Mexico, and every now and then passed a straw-thatched
jacal, where women sat selling "atole," that is a kind of stir-
about of pine-nut meal and milk, and dishes seasoned hot
with red pepper, with tortillas made on the metate of the
Aztecs, to serve as bread and spoons. The infidels, it seemed,
had got ahead of us, and when we slept had been descried
making towards the north; two of them armed with bows
which they had roughly made with sticks, the string twisted
out of istle, and the rest with clubs, and what astonished me
most was that behind them trotted a white dog. Outside
San Juan del Rio, which we reached upon the second day,
it seemed that in the night the homing Mescaleros had stolen
a horse, and two of them mounting upon him had ridden off,
leaving the rest of the forlorn and miserable band behind.
How they had lived so far in the scorched alkali-covered
plains, how they managed to conceal themselves by day, or
how they steered by night, no one could tell; for the interior
Mexican knows nothing of the desert craft, and has no idea
that there is always food of some kind for an Apache, either
by digging roots, snaring small animals, or at the last resort
by catching locusts or any other insect he can find. Nothing
so easy as to conceal themselves; for amongst grass eight or
nine inches high, they drop, and in an instant, even as you
look, are lost to sight, and if hard pressed sometimes
escape attention by standing in a cactus grove, and,
stretching out their arms, look so exactly like the plant that

you may pass close to them and be unaware, till their bow twangs, and an obsidian-headed arrow whistles through the air.

Our caravan rested a day outside San Juan del Rio to shoe the mules, repair the harness, and for the muleteers to go to mass or visit the poblana girls, who with flowers in their hair leaned out of every balcony of the half-Spanish, half-Oriental-looking town, according to their taste. Not that the halt lost time, for travellers all know that "to hear mass and to give barley to your beasts loses no tittle of the day."

San Juan, the river almost dry, and trickling thirstily under its red stone bridges; the fields of aloes, the poplars, and the stunted palms; its winding street in which the houses, over-hanging, almost touch; its population, which seemed to pass their time lounging wrapped in striped blankets up against the walls, was left behind. The pulque-aloes and the sugar-canes grew scarcer, the road more desolate as we emerged into the "tierra fría" of the central plain, and all the time the Sierra Madre, jagged and menacing, towered in the west. In my mind's eye I saw the Mescaleros trotting like wolves all through the night along its base, sleeping by day in holes, killing a sheep or goat when chance occurred, and following one another silent and stoical in their tramp towards the north.

Days followed days as in a ship at sea; the wagons rolling on across the plains; and I jogging upon my horse, half sleeping in the sun, or stretched at night half dozing on a tilt, almost lost count of time. Somewhere between San Juan del Rio and San Luis Potosi we learned two of the Indians had been killed, but that the four remaining were still pushing onward, and in a little while we met a body of armed men carrying two ghastly heads tied by their scalp-locks to the saddle-bow. Much did the slayers vaunt their prowess; telling how in a word at break of day they had fallen in with all the Indians seated round a fire, and that whilst the rest fled, two had sprung on them, as they said, "after the fashion of wild beasts, armed one with a stick, and the other with a stone, and by God's grace," and here the leader crossed himself, "their aim had been successful, and the two sons of dogs had fallen, but most unfortunately the rest during the fight had managed to escape."

San Luis Potosi, the rainless city, once world-renowned for wealth, and even now full of fine buildings, churches and palaces, and with a swarming population of white-clothed Indians squatting to sell their trumpery in the great market-square, loomed up amongst its fringe of gardens, irrigated lands, its groves of pepper trees, its palms, its wealth of flowering shrubs; its great white domes, giving an air of Bagdad or of Fez, shone in the distance, then grew nearer, and at last swallowed us up, as wearily we passed through the outskirts of the town, and halted underneath the walls.

The city, then an oasis in the vast plateau of Anahuac (now but a station on a railway-line), a city of enormous distances, of gurgling water led in stucco channels by the side of every street, of long expanses of adobe walls, of immense plazas, of churches and of bells, of countless convents; hedged in by mountains to the west, mouth of the "tierra caliente" to the east, and to the north the stopping-place for the long trains of wagons carrying cotton from the States; wrapped in a mist as of the Middle Ages, lay sleeping in the sun. On every side the plain lapped like an ocean, and the green vegetation round the town stopped so abruptly that you could step almost at once from fertile meadows into a waste of whitish alkali.

Above the town, in a foothill of the Sierra Madre about three leagues away, is situated the "Enchanted City," never yet fouled by the foot of man, but yet existent, and believed in by all those who follow that best part of history, the traditions which have come down to us from the times when men were wise, and when imagination governed judgment, as it should do to-day, being the noblest faculty of the human mind. Either want of time, or that belittling education from

which few can escape, prevented me from visiting the place.
Yet I still think, if rightly sought, the city will be found, and
I feel sure the Mescaleros passed the night not far from it,
and perhaps looking down upon San Luis Potosi cursed it,
after the fashion that the animals may curse mankind for its
injustice to them.

Tired of its squares, its long dark streets, its hum of people;
and possessed perhaps with that nostalgia of the desert which
comes so soon to all who once have felt its charm when
cooped in bricks, we set our faces northward about an hour
before the day, passed through the gates and rolled into the
plains. The mules well rested shook their bells, the leagues
soon dropped behind, the muleteers singing "La Pasadita,"
or an interminable song about a "Gachupin"* who loved
a nun.

The Mescaleros had escaped our thoughts—that is, the
muleteers thought nothing of them; but I followed their every
step, saw them crouched round their little fire, roasting the
roots of wild mescal; marked them upon the march in single
file, their eyes fixed on the plain, watchful and silent as they
were phantoms gliding to the north.

Crossing a sandy tract, the Capataz, who had long lived in
the Pimeria Alta, and amongst the Maricopas on the Gila,
drew up his horse and pointing to the ground said: "Viva
Mexico!—look at these footmarks in the sand. They are the
infidels; see where the men have trod; here is the woman's
print and this the boy's. Look how their toes are all turned
in, unlike the tracks of Christians. This trail is a day old,
and yet how fresh! See where the boy has stumbled—thanks
to the Blessed Virgin they must all be tired, and praise to
God will die upon the road, either by hunger or some
Christian hand." All that he spoke of was no doubt visible
to him, but through my want of faith, or perhaps lack of
experience, I saw but a faint trace of naked footsteps in the

* It had a chorus reflecting upon convent discipline:
        "For though the convent rule was strict and tight,
        She had her exits and her entrances by night."

sand. Such as they were, they seemed the shadow of a ghost, unstable and unreal, and struck me after the fashion that it strikes one when a man holds up a cane and tells you gravely, without a glimmering of the strangeness of the fact, that it came from Japan, actually grew there, and had leaves and roots, and was as little thought of as a mere ash-plant growing in a copse.

At an hacienda upon the road, just where the trail leads off upon one hand to Matehuala, and on the other to Rio Verde, and the hot countries of the coast, we stopped to pass the hottest hours in sleep. All was excitement; men came in, their horses flecked with foam; others were mounting, and all armed to the teeth, as if the Yankees had crossed the Rio Grande, and were marching on the place. "Los Indios! sí, señor," they had been seen, only last night, but such the valour of the people of the place, they had passed on doing no further damage than to kill a lamb. No chance of sleep in such a turmoil of alarm; each man had his own plan, all talked at once, most of them were half drunk, and when our Capataz asked dryly if they had thought of following the trail, a silence fell on all. By this time, owing to the horsemen galloping about, the trail was cut on every side, and to have followed it would have tried the skill of an Apache tracker; but just then upon the plain a cloud of dust was seen. Nearer it came, and then out of the midst of it horses appeared, arms flashed, and then nearing the place five or six men galloped up to the walls, and stopped their horses with a jerk. "What news? Have you seen anything of the Apaches?" and the chief rider of the gallant band, getting off slowly, and fastening up his horse, said, with an air of dignity: "At the encrucijada, four leagues along the road, you will find one of them. We came upon him sitting on a stone, too tired to move, called on him to surrender, but Indians have no sense, so he came at us tired as he was, and we, being valiant, fired, and he fell dead. Then, that the law should be made manifest to all, we hung his body by

the feet to a huisaché tree." Then compliments broke out
and "Vivan los valientes!" "Viva Mexico!" "Mueran los
Indios salvajes!" and much of the same sort, whilst the five
valiant men modestly took a drink, saying but little, for true
courage does not show itself in talk.

Leaving the noisy crew drinking confusion to their enemies, we rolled into the plain. Four dusty leagues, and the
huisaché tree growing by four cross trails came into sight.
We neared it, and to a branch, naked except his breech-clout,
covered with bullet-wounds, we saw the Indian hang. Half-
starved he looked, and so reduced that from the bullet-holes
but little blood had run; his feet were bloody, and his face
hanging an inch or two above the ground distorted; flies
buzzed about him, and in the sky a faint black line on the
horizon showed that the vultures had already scented food.

We left the nameless warrior hanging on his tree, and
took our way across the plain, well pleased both with the
"valour" of his slayers and the position of affairs in general
in the world at large. Right up and down the Rio Grande
on both sides for almost a thousand miles the lonely cross
upon some riverside, near to some thicket, or out in the wide
plain, most generally is lettered "Killed by the Apaches,"
and in the game they played so long, and still held trumps
in at the time I write of, they too paid for all errors, in their
play, by death. But still it seemed a pity, savage as they were,
that so much cunning, such stoical indifference to both death
and life, should always finish as the warrior whom I saw hang
by the feet from the huisaché, just where the road to Matehuala bifurcates, and the trail breaks off to El Jarral. And so
we took our road, passed La Parida, Matehuala, El Catorce,
and still the sterile plateau spread out like a vast sea, the
sparse and stunted bushes in the constant mirage looming
at times like trees, at others seeming just to float above the
sand; and as we rolled along, the mules struggling and
straining in the whitish dust, we seemed to lose all trace of
the Apaches; and at the lone hacienda or rare villages no one

had heard of them, and the mysterious hegira of the party, now reduced to three, left no more traces of its passing than water which has closed upon the passage of a fish.

Gomez Farias, Parras, El Llano de la Guerra, we passed alternately, and at length Saltillo came in sight, its towers standing up upon the plain after the fashion of a lighthouse in the sea; the bull-ring built under the Viceroys looking like a fort; and then the plateau of Anahuac finished abruptly, and from the ramparts of the willow-shaded town the great green plains stretched out towards Texas in a vast panorama; whilst upon the west in the dim distance frowned the serrated mountains of Santa Rosa, and further still the impenetrable fastnesses of the Bolson de Mapimi.

Next day we took the road for Monterey, descending in a day by the rough path known as "la cuesta de los fierros," from the cold plateau to a land of palms, of cultivation, orange groves, of fruit trees, olive gardens, a balmy air filled with the noise of running waters; and passing underneath the Cerro de la Silla which dominates the town, slept peacefully far from all thoughts of Indians and of perils of the road, in the great caravansary which at that time was the chief glory of the town of Monterey. The city with its shady streets, its alameda planted with palm trees, and its plaza all decorated with stuccoed plaster seats painted pale pink, and upon which during both day and night half of the population seemed to lounge, lay baking in the sun.

Great teams of wagons driven by Texans creaked through the streets, the drivers dressed in a défroque of old town clothes, often a worn frock-coat and rusty trousers stuffed into cowboy boots, the whole crowned with an ignominious battered hat, and looking, as the Mexicans observed, like "pantomimas, que salen en las fiestas." Mexicans from down the coast, from Tamaulipas, Tuxpan, Vera Cruz and Guatzecoalcos ambled along on horses all ablaze with silver; and to complete the picture, a tribe of Indians, the Kickapoos, who had migrated from the north, and who occasionally rode through the town in single file, their rifles in their hands, and looking at the shops half longingly, half frightened, passed along without a word.

But all the varied peoples, the curious half-wild, half-patriarchal life, the fruits and flowers, the strangeness of the place, could not divert my thoughts from the three lone pathetic figures, followed by their dog, which in my mind's eye I saw making northward, as a wild goose finds its path in spring, leaving no traces of its passage by the way. I wondered what they thought of, how they looked upon the world, if they respected all they saw of civilized communities upon their way, or whether they pursued their journey like a horse let loose returning to his birthplace, anxious alone about arriving at the goal. So Monterey became a memory; the Cerro de la Silla last vanishing, when full five leagues upon the road. The dusty plains all white with alkali, the grey-green sage-bushes, the salt and crystal-looking rivers, the Indians bending under burdens, and the women sitting at the cross-roads selling tortillas—all now had changed. Through oceans of tall grass, by muddy rivers in which alligators basked, by bayous, resacas, and by "bottoms" of alluvial soil, in which grew cotton-woods, black-jack, and post-oak, with gigantic willows; through countless herds of half-wild horses, lighting the landscape with their colours, and through a rolling prairie with vast horizons bounded by faint blue mountain chains, we took our way. Out of the thickets of mezquite wild boars peered upon the path; rattle-snakes sounded their note of warning or lay basking in the sun; at times an antelope bounded across our track, and the rare villages were fortified with high mud walls, had gates and sometimes drawbridges, for all the country we were passing through was subject to invasions of "los indios bravos," and no one rode a mile without the chance of an attack. When travellers met they zigzagged to and fro like battleships in the old days striving to get the "weather gauge," holding their horses tightly by the head, and interchanging salutations fifty yards away, though if they happened to be Texans and Mexicans they only glared, or perhaps yelled an obscenity at one another in their different tongues. Advertisements upon the trees informed the traveller that the place to stop at was the "Old Buffalo Camp" in San Antonio, setting forth its whisky, its perfect safety both for man and beast, and adding curtly it was only a short four hundred miles away. Here for the first time in our journey we sent out a rider about half a mile ahead to scan the route, ascend the little hills, keep a sharp eye on "Indian sign," and give us warning by a timely shot, all to dismount, corral the wagons, and be prepared for an attack of Indians, or of the roaming bands of rascals who like pirates wandered on the plains. Dust made us anxious, and smoke ascending in the distance set us all wondering if it was Indians, or a shepherd's fire; at halting time no one strayed far from camp, and we sat eating with our rifles by our sides, whilst men on horseback rode round the mules, keeping them well in sight, as shepherds watch their sheep. About two leagues from Juarez a traveller bloody with spurring passed us carrying something in his hand; he stopped and held out a long arrow with an obsidian head, painted in various colours, and feathered in a peculiar way. A consultation found it to be "Apache," and the man galloped on to take it to the governor of the place to tell him Indians were about, or, as he shouted (following the old Spanish catchword), "there were Moors upon the coast."

Juarez we slept at, quite secure within the walls; started at daybreak, crossing the swiftly running river just outside the town, at the first streak of light; journeyed all day, still hearing nothing of the retreating Mescaleros, and before evening reached Las Navas, which we found astir, all lighted up, and knots of people talking excitedly, whilst in the plaza the whole population seemed to be afoot. At the long wooden tables set about with lights, where in a Mexican town at sundown an al fresco meal of kid stewed in red pepper, tamales and tortillas, is always laid, the talk was furious, and each man gave his opinion at the same time, after the fashion of the Russian mir, or as it may be that we shall yet see done during debates in Parliament, so that all men may have a chance to speak, and yet escape the ignominy of their words being caught, set down, and used against them, after the present plan. The Mescaleros had been seen passing about a league outside the town. A shepherd lying hidden, watching his sheep, armed with a rifle, had spied them, and reported that they had passed close to him; the woman coming last and carrying in her arms a little dog; and he "thanked God and all His holy saints who had miraculously preserved his life." After the shepherd's story, in the afternoon firing had been distinctly heard towards the small rancho of Las Crucecitas, which lay about three leagues further on upon the road. All night the din of talk went on, and in the morning when we started on our way, full half the population went with us to the gate, all giving good advice; to keep a good look-out, if we saw dust to be certain it was Indians driving the horses stolen from Las Crucecitas, then to get off at once, corral the wagons, and above all to put our trust in God. This we agreed to do, but wondered why out of so many valiant men not one of them proffered assistance, or volunteered to mount his horse and ride with us along the dangerous way.

The road led upwards towards some foothills, set about with scrubby palms; not fifteen miles away rose the dark mountains of the Santa Rosa chain, and on a little hill the rancho stood, flat-roofed and white, and seemingly not more than a short league away, so clear the light, and so immense the scale of everything upon the rolling plain. I knew that in the mountains the three Indians were safe, as the whole range was Indian territory; and as I saw them struggling up the slopes, the little dog following them footsore, hanging down its head, or carried as the shepherd said in the "she-devil's" arms, I wished them luck after their hegira, planned with such courage, carried out so well, had ended, and they were back again amongst the tribe.

Just outside Crucecitas we met a Texan who, as he told us, owned the place, and lived in "kornkewbinage with a native gal," called, as he said, "Pastory," who it appeared of all females he had ever met was the best hand to bake "tortillers," and whom, had she not been a Catholic, he would have made his wife. All this without a question on our part, and sitting sideways on his horse, scanning the country from the corner of his eye. He told us that he had "had right smart of an Indian trouble here yesterday just about afternoon. Me and my 'vaquerys' were around looking for an estray horse, just six of us, when close to the ranch we popped kermash right upon three red devjls, and opened fire at once. I hed a Winchester, and at the first fire tumbled the buck; he fell right in his tracks, and jest as I was taking off his scalp, I'm dog-goned if the squaw and the young devil didn't come at us jest like grizzly bars. Wal, yes, killed 'em, o' course, and anyhow the young 'un would have growed up; but the squaw I'm sort of sorry about. I never could bear to kill a squaw, though I've often seen it done. Naow here's the all-firedest thing yer ever heard; jes' as I was turning the bodies over with my foot a little Indian dog flies at us like a 'painter,' the varmint, the condemndest little buffler I ever struck. I was for shootin' him, but Pastory—that's my kornkewbyne—she up and says it was a shame. Wal, we had to bury them, for dead Injun stinks worse than turkey-buzzard, and the dodgasted little dog is sitting on the grave, 'pears like he's froze, leastwise he hasn't moved since sun-up, when we planted the whole crew."

Under a palm tree not far from the house the Indians' grave was dug; upon it, wretched and draggled, sat the little dog. "Pastory" tried to catch it all day long, being kind-hearted though a "kornkewbyne"; but, failing, said "God was not willing," and retired into the house. The hours seemed days in the accursed place till the sun rose, gilding the unreached Santa Rosa mountains, and bringing joy into the world. We harnessed up the mules, and started silently out on the lonely road; turning, I checked my horse, and began moralizing on all kinds of things; upon tenacity of purpose, the futility of life, and the inexorable fate which mocks mankind, making all effort useless, whilst still urging us to strive. Then the grass rustled, and across an open space a small white object trotted, looking furtively around, threw up its head and howled, ran to and fro as if it sought for something, howled dismally again, and after scratching in the ground, squatted dejectedly on the fresh-turned-up earth which marked the Indians' grave.

THE CAPTIVE

SOMEHOW or other none of the camp could sleep that night. It may have been that they were hungry, for they were just returning from a bootless attempt to overtake a band of Indians who had carried off the horses from an *estancia** on the Napostá. Night had fallen on them just by the crossing of a river, where a small grove of willows had given them sufficient wood to make a fire, for nothing is more cheerless than the fierce transient flame ("like a nun's love") that cow-dung and dry thistle-stems afford. Although they had not eaten since the morning, when they had finished their last strips of *charqui*,† they had a little *yerba*,‡ and so sat by the fire passing the *mate*§ round and smoking black Brazilian cigarettes.

The stream, either a fork of the Mostazas or the head waters of the Napostá itself, ran sluggishly between its banks of rich alluvial soil. Just at the crossing it was poached into thick mud by half-wild cattle and by herds of mares, for no one rode where they were camped in those days but the Indians, and only they when they came in to burn the settlements. A cow or two which had gone in to drink and remained in the mud to die, their eyes picked out by the *caranchos*,‖ lay swelled to an enormous size, and with their legs sticking out grotesquely, just as a soldier's dead legs stick out upon a battlefield.

From the still, starry night the mysterious noises of the desert rose, cattle coughed dryly as they stood on rising ground, and now and then a stallion whinnied as he rounded

*Estancia—estate.
†*Charqui*—dried meat.
‡*Yerba*—Paraquayan tea leaves.
§*Mate*—the gourd in which *yerba* is served.
‖*Caranchos*—birds resembling hawks.

44

up his mares. *Vizcachas** uttered their sharp bark and
tuco-tucos† sounded their metallic chirp deep underneath the
ground. The flowers of the *chañar* gave out their spicy scent
in the night air, and out beyond the clumps of *piquillin* and
molle, the pampa grass upon the river-bank looked like a
troop of ostriches in the moon's dazzling rays.

The Southern Cross was hung above their heads, Capella
was just rising, and from a planet a yellow beam of light
seemed to fall into the rolling waves of grass, which the
light wind just stirred, sending a ghostly murmur through it,
as if the sound of surf upon some sea which had evaporated
thousands of years ago was echoing in the breeze.

A line of sand-hills ran beside the stream. Below their
white and silvery sides the horses, herded by a man who
now and then rode slowly to the fire to light a cigarette,
grazed on the wiry grass. The tinkling bells of the *madrinas*
(bell-mares) had been muffled, as there was still a chance the
Indians might have cut the trail, and now and then the horse
guard cautiously crawled up the yielding bank and gazed
out on the plain, which in the moonlight looked like a
frozen lake.

Grouped round the fire were most of the chief settlers on
the *Sauce Grande*, *Mostazas*, and the *Napostá*.

The brothers Milburn, who had been merchant sailors,
dressed in cord breeches and brown riding-boots, but
keeping, as it were, a link with ships in their serge coats,
were there, sitting up squarely, smoking and spitting in
the fire.

Next to them sat Martin Villalba, a wealthy cattle-farmer
and major in the militia of Bahía Blanca. No one had ever
seen him in his uniform, although he always wore a sword
stuck underneath the girth of his *recao* (saddle). The light
shone on his Indian features and was reflected back from his
long hair, which hung upon his shoulders as black and glossy

* *Vizcachas*—animals resembling prairie dogs.
† *tuco-tucos*—a kind of mole.

as the feathers of a crow. As he sat glaring at the blaze he now and then put up his hand and listened, and as he did so, all the rest of those assembled listened as well, the man who had the *mate* in his hand holding it in suspense until Villalba silently shook his head, or murmuring: "It is nothing," began to talk again. Spaniards and Frenchmen sat side by side with an Italian, one Enrique Clerici, who had served with Garibaldi in his youth, but now was owner of a *pulpería* (pampa store) that he had named "The Rose of the South," and in it hung a picture of his quondam leader, which he referred to as "my saint."

Claraz, the tall, black-bearded Swiss, was there. He had lost one finger by a tiger's bite in Paraguay, and was a quiet, meditative man who had roamed all the continent, from Acapulco down to Punta Arenas, and hoped some day to publish an exhaustive work upon the flora of the Pampa, when, as he said, he found a philanthropic publisher to undertake the loss.

The German, Friedrich Vögel, was bookkeeper at an *estancia* called *La Casa de Fierro*, but being young and a good horseman had joined the others, making a contrast to them as he sat beside the fire in his town clothes, which, though they were all dusty and his trouser-legs coated thick with mud, yet gave him the appearance of being on a picnic, which a small telescope that dangled from a strap greatly accentuated. Since he had started on the trail eight or nine days ago, he had Hispaniolised his name to Pancho Pájaro, which form, as fortune willed it, stuck to him for the remainder of his life in South America. Two cattle-farmers, English by nationality, known as *El Facon Grande* and *El Facón Chico* from the respective sizes of the knives they carried, talked quietly, just as they would have talked in the bow-window of a club, whilst a tall, grey-haired Belgian, handsome and taciturn, was drawing horses' brands with a charred mutton-bone as he sat gazing in the fire. Of all the company he alone kept himself apart, speaking but seldom, and though he had passed a lifetime on the plains, he never adventured his opinion except men asked for it, when it was taken usually as final, for everybody knew that he had served upon the frontier under old General Mancilla in the Indian wars.

A tall, fair English boy, whose hair, as curly as the wool of a merino sheep, hung round his face and on his neck after the fashion of a Charles II wig, was nodding sleepily.

Exaltación Medina, tall, thin and wiry, tapped with his whip upon his boot-leg, on which an eagle was embroidered in red silk.

He and his friend, Florencio Freites, who sat and picked his teeth abstractedly with his long silver-handled knife, were gauchos of the kind who always rode good horses and wore good clothes, though no one ever saw them work, except occasionally at cattle-marketings. They both were *Badilleros*, that is, men from Bahía Blanca, and both spoke Araucano,* having been prisoners amongst the Infidel, for their misfortunes as they said, although there were not wanting people who averred that their connection with the Indians had been in the capacity of renegades by reason of their crimes.

Some squatted cross-legged like a Turk, and some lay resting on their elbows, whilst others, propped against their saddles, sat with their eyes closed, but opened them if the wind stirred the trees, just as a sleeping cat peers through its eyelids at an unusual noise.

When the last *mate* had been drunk and the last cigarette end flung into the blazing brands and yet a universal sleeplessness seemed to hang in the air, which came in fierce, hot gusts out of the north, carrying with it a thousand cottony filaments which clung upon the hair and beards of the assembled band, Claraz suggested that it might be as well if someone would tell a story, for it was plain that, situated as they were, no one could sing a song. Silence fell on the group, for most of those assembled there had stories that they did not care to tell. Then the mysterious impulse that invariably directs

*The language of the Arancano Indians.

men's gaze towards the object of their thoughts turned every eye upon the Belgian, who still was drawing brands on the white ashes of the fire with the burnt mutton-bone. Raising his head he said: "I see I am the man you wish to tell the story, and as I cannot sleep an atom better than the rest, and as the story I will tell you lies on my heart like lead, but in the telling may perhaps grow lighter, I will begin at once."

He paused, and taking off his hat, ran his hands through his thick, dark hair, flecked here and there with grey, hitched round his pistol so that it should not stick into his side as he leaned on his elbow, and turning to the fire, which shone upon his face, set in a close-cut, dark-brown beard, slowly began to speak.

"Fifteen—no, wasn't it almost sixteen years ago—just at the time of the great Indian, Malon—invasion, eh? the time they got as far as Tapalquén and burned the *chacras* (farms) just outside Tandil, I was living on the Sauce Chico, quite on the frontier. . . . I used to drive my horses into the corral at night and sleep with a Winchester on either side of me. My nearest neighbour was a countryman of mine, young . . . yes, I think you would have called him a young man then. An educated man, quiet and well-mannered, yes, I think that was so . . . his manners were not bad.

"It is his story I shall tell you, not mine, you know. Somehow or other I think it was upon an expedition after the Indians, such as ours to-day, he came upon an Indian woman driving some horses. She had got separated from her husband after some fight or other, and was returning to the tents. She might have got away, as she was riding a good horse . . . piebald it was, with both its ears slit, and the cartilage between the nose divided to give it better wind. Curious the superstitions that they have." Florencio Freites looked at the speaker, nodded and interjected: "If you had lived with them as long as I have you would say so, my friend. I would give something to slit the cartilage of some of their

48

Indian snouts. . . . " No one taking up what he had said,
he settled down to listen, and the narrator once again
began.

"Yes, a fine horse that piebald, I knew him well, a little
quick to mount, but then that woman rode like a gaucho—
as well as any man. As I was saying, she might have got
away—so said my friend—only the mare of her *tropilla*
(troop) had not long foaled, and either she was hard to drive
or the maternal instinct in the woman was too strong for her
to leave the foal behind . . . or she had lost her head or
something—you can never tell. When my friend took her
prisoner, she did not fight or try to get away, but looked at
him and said in halting Spanish: 'Bueno, I am take prisoner,
do what you like.' My friend looked at her and saw that she
was young and pretty, and that her hair was brown and curly,
and fell down to her waist. Perhaps he thought—God knows
what he did think. For one thing, he had no woman in his
house, for the last, an Italian girl from Buenos Aires, had
run off with a countryman of her own, who came round
selling saints—a *santero*, eh? As he looked at her, her eyes
fell, and he could have sworn he saw the colour rise under
the paint daubed on her face, but he said nothing as they
rode back towards his rancho, apart from all the rest. They
camped upon the head waters of the Quequén Salado, and
to my friend's astonishment, when he had staked out his
horse and hers and put the hobbles on her mare, so that her
tropilla might not stray, she had lit the fire and put a little
kettle on to boil. When they had eaten some tough *charqui*
(dried meat), moistened in warm water, she handed him a
mate and stood submissively filling it for him till he had had
enough. Two or three times he looked at her, but mastered
his desire to ask her how it was that she spoke Spanish and
why her hair was brown.

"As they sat looking at the fire, it seemed somehow as if
he had known her all his life, and when a voice came from
another fire, 'You had better put the hobbles on that Indian

mare, or she'll be back to the *querencia** before the moon is down,' it jarred on him, for somehow he vaguely knew his captive would not try to run away.

"So with a shout of 'All right, I'll look out,' to the other fires, he took his saddle and his ponchos, and saying to the Indian woman, 'Sleep well, we start at daybreak,' left her wrapped up in saddle-cloths, with her feet towards the fire. An hour before the dawn the camp was all astir, but my friend, though an early riser, found his captive ready, and waiting with a *mate* for him, as soon as he got up and shook the dew out of his hair, and buckled on his spurs.

"All that day they rode homewards, companions leaving them at intervals, as when they struck the Saucecito, crossed the Mostazas, just as it rises at the foot of the Sierra de la Ventana, or at the ruined rancho at the head waters of the Napostá. Generally, as the various neighbours drove their *tropillas* off, they turned and shouted farewell to the Indian woman and my friend, wishing them a happy honeymoon or something of the kind. He answered shortly, and she never appeared to hear, although he saw that she had understood. Before they reached his rancho he had learned a little of the history of the woman riding by his side. She told him, as Spanish slowly seemed to make its way back to her brain, that she was eight-and-twenty, and her father had been an *estanciero* (the owner of a ranch) in the province of San Luis; who with her mother and her brothers had been killed in an invasion of the Indians eight years ago, and from that time she had lived with them, and had been taken by a chief whose name was Huinchan, by whom she had three sons. All this she told my friend mechanically, as if she had been speaking of another, adding: 'The Christian women pass through hell amongst the *Infidel*.' " The narrator paused to take a *mate*, and Anastasio sententiously remarked: "Hell, yes, double-heated hell: do you remember, Ché, that Chilian girl you bought from that Araucan whose eye one of the Indian girls

Querencia—a horse's home region.

gouged out?" His friend Florencio showed his teeth like a wolf and answered: "Caspita, yes; do you remember how I got even with her? Eye for an eye, tooth for a tooth, as I once heard a priest say was God's law!" The *mate* finished, the Belgian once again took up his tale.

"When my friend reached his home he helped his captive off her horse, hobbled her mare, and taking her hand led her into the house and told her it was hers.

"She was the least embarrassed of the two, and from the first took up her duties as if she had never known another life.

"Little by little she laid aside her Indian dress and ways, although she folded carefully and laid by her *chamál*, with the great silver pin shaped like a sun that holds it tight across the breast. Her ear-rings, shaped like an inverted pyramid, she put aside with the scarlet *fichú* that had bound her hair, which when she was first taken hung down her back in a thick mass of curls that had resisted all the efforts of the Indian women, aided by copious dressings of melted ostrich fat, to make straight like their own. Timidly she had asked for Christian clothes, and by degrees became again a Spanish woman, careful about her hair, which she wore high upon her head, careful about her shoes, and by degrees her walk became again the walk she had practised in her youth, when with her mother she had sauntered in the evening through the plaza of her native town, with a light swinging of her hips.

"Her Indian name of Lincomilla gave place once more to Nievés, and in a week or two some of the sunburn vanished from her cheeks.

"All the time of her transformation my friend watched the process as a man may watch the hour-hand on a clock, knowing it moves, but yet unable to discern the movement with his eyes.

"Just as it seems a miracle when on a fine spring morning one wakes and sees a tree which overnight was bare, now crowned with green, so did it seem a miracle to him that the half-naked Indian whom he had captured, swinging her whip about her head and shouting to her horses, had turned into the Señorita Nievés, whilst he had barely seen the change. Something intangible seemed to have grown up between them, invisible, but quite impossible to pass, and now and then he caught himself regretting vaguely that he had let his captive slip out of his hands. Little by little their positions were reversed, and he who had been waited on by Lincomilla found himself treating the Señorita Nievés with all the . . . how you say . . . '*égards*' that a man uses to a lady in ordinary life.

"When his hand accidentally touched hers he shivered, and then cursed himself for a fool for not having taken advantage of the right of conquest the first day that he led the Indian girl into his home. All would have then seemed natural, and he would have only had another girl to serve his *mate*, a link in the long line of women who had succeeded one another since he first drove his cattle into the south camps and built his rancho on the creek. Then came a time when something seemed to blot out all the world, and nothing mattered but the Señorita Nievés, whom he desired so fiercely that his heart stood still when she brushed past him in her household duties; yet he refrained from speaking, kept back by pride, for he knew that, after all, she was in his power in that lone rancho on the plains. Sleeping and waking she was always there. If he rode out upon the *boleada** she seemed to go with him; on his return there she was standing, waiting for him with her enigmatic smile when he came home at night.

"She on her side was quite aware of all he suffered, suffering herself just as acutely, but being able better to conceal her feelings he never noticed it, or saw the shadowy look that long-suppressed desire brings in a woman's eyes. Their neighbours, ordinary men and women, had no idea

*A hunt with the bolas.

things were on such an exalted footing, and openly con-
gratulated him on his good luck in having caught an Indian
who had turned to a white girl. When he had heard these
rough congratulations on his luck, he used to answer shortly,
and catching his horse by the head, would gallop out upon
the plain and come home tired, but with the same pain
gnawing at his heart. How long they might have gone on
in that way is hard to say, had not the woman—for it is
generally they who take the first step in such things—
suddenly put an end to it. Seeing him sitting by the fire one
evening, and having watched him follow her with his eyes
as she came in and out, she walked up to him and laid her
hand upon his shoulder, and as he started and a thrill ran
through his veins, bent down her face and pressing her dry
lips to his, said: 'Take me,' and slid into his arms.

"That was their courtship. From that time, all up and
down the Sauce Chico, the settlers, who looked on love as
a thing men wrote about in books, or as the accomplishment
of a necessary function without which no society could
possibly endure, took a proprietary interest in the lovers,
whom they called 'Los de Teruel,' after the lovers in the old
Spanish play, who loved so constantly.

"Most certainly they loved as if they had invented love
and meant to keep it to themselves. Foolish, of course they
were, and primitive, he liking to rush off into Bahía Blanca
to buy up all the jewellery that he could find to give her,
and she, forgetting all the horrors of her life amongst the
Indians, gave herself up to happiness as unrestrained as that
of our first mother, when the whole world contained no other
man but the one she adored.

"As in a day out on the southern plains, when all is still
and the wild horses play, and from the lakes long lines of
pink flamingoes rise into the air and seem translucent in the
sun, when the whole sky becomes intensest purple, throwing
a shadow on the grass that looks as if the very essence of
the clouds was falling like a dew, the Indians say that a

Pampero must be brewing, and will soon burst with devastating force upon the happy world, so did their love presage misfortune by its intensity."

"A strong north wind is sure to bring a pampero,"* interpolated one of the listeners round the fire.

"Yes, that is so, and the pampero came accordingly," rejoined the story-teller.

"Months passed and still the neighbours talked of them with amazement, being used to see the force of passion burn itself out, just as a fire burns out in straw, and never having heard of any other kind of love except the sort they and their animals enjoyed.

"Then by degrees Nievés became a little melancholy, and used to sit for hours looking out on the pampa, and then come in and hide her head beneath her black Manila shawl, that shawl my friend had galloped to Bahía Blanca to procure, and had returned within two days, doing the forty leagues at a round gallop all the way.

"Little by little he became alarmed, and feared, having been a man whose own affections in the past had often strayed, that she was tired of him. To all his questions she invariably replied that she had been supremely happy, and for the first time had known love, which she had always thought was but a myth invented by the poets to pass the time away. Then she would cry and say that he was idiotic to doubt her for a moment, then catching him to her, crush him against her heart. For days together she was cheerful, but he, after the fashion of a man who thinks he has detected a slight lameness in his horse, but is not certain where, was always on the watch to try and find out what it was that ailed her, till gradually a sort of armed neutrality took the place of their love. Neither would speak, although both suffered almost as much as they had loved, until one evening as they stood looking out upon the Pampa yearning for one another, but kept apart by something that they felt, rather

*Pampero—a stormy south wind.

than knew was there, the woman with a cry threw herself into her lover's arms. Then with an effort she withdrew herself, and choking down her tears, said: 'I have been happy, dearest, happier by far than you can understand, happier than I think it is ever possible to be for any man. Think of my life, my father and my mother killed before my eyes, myself thrown to an Indian whom my soul loathed, then made by force the mother of his children—his and mine. Think what my life has been there in the *tolderías* (colony of Indian tents), exposed to the jealousy of all the Indian women, always in danger till my sons were born, and even then obliged to live for years amongst those savages and become as themselves.

" 'Then you came, and it seemed to me as if God had tired of persecuting me; but now I find that He or nature has something worse in store. I am happy here, but then there is no happiness on earth, I think. My children—his and mine—never cease calling me. I must return to them— and see, my horses all are fat, the foal can travel, and . . . you must think it has been all a dream, and let me go back to my master—husband—bear him more children, and at last be left to die when I am old, beside some river, like other Indian wives.' She dried her eyes, and gently touching him upon the shoulder, looked at him sadly, saying: 'Now you know, dearest, why it is I have been so sad and made you suffer, though you have loaded me with love. Now that you know I love you more a hundred times than the first day when, as you used to say, I took you for my own, you can let me go back to my duties and my misery, and perhaps understand.'

"Her lover saw her mind was fixed, and with an effort stammered: 'Bueno, you were my prisoner, but ever since I took you captive I have been your slave. . . . When will you go?'

"Let it be to-morrow, *sangre mía* (my blood), and at daybreak, for you must take me to the place where you first saw me; it has become to me as it were a birthplace, seeing that there I first began to live.' Once more he answered, '*Bueno*,' like a man in a dream, and led her sadly back into their house.

"Just as the first red streaks of the false dawn had tinged the sky they saddled up without a word.

"Weary and miserable, with great black circles round their eyes, they stood a moment, holding their horses by their *cabrestos* (lead ropes), till the rising sun just fell upon the doorway of the poor rancho where they had been so happy in their love.

"Without a word they mounted, the captive once more turned to Lincomilla, dressed in her Indian clothes, swinging herself as lightly to the saddle as a man. Then gathering the horses all together, with the foal, now strong and fat, running behind its mother, they struck into the plains.

"Three or four hours of steady galloping brought them close to the place where Lincomilla had been taken captive by him who now rode silently beside her, with his eyes fixed on the horizon, like a man in a dream.

" 'It should be here,' she said, 'close to that tuft of *sarandís* . . . yes, there it is, for I remember it was there you took my horse by the bridle, as if you thought that I was sure to run away, back to the Indians.'

"Dismounting, they talked long and sadly, till Lincomilla tore herself from her lover's arms and once more swung herself upon her horse. The piebald Pingo with the split ears neighed shrilly to the other horses feeding a little distance off upon the plain, then, just as she raised her hand to touch his mouth, the man she was about to leave for ever stooped down and kissed her foot, which rested naked on the stirrup, after the Indian style. 'May the God of the Araucans, to whom you go, bless and encompass you,' he cried; 'my God has failed me,' and as he spoke she touched her horse lightly with the long Indian reins. The piebald plunged and wheeled round, and then struck into a measured gallop, as his rider, gathering her horses up before her, set her face westward, without once looking back.

"I . . . that is my friend, stood gazing at her, watching the driven horses first sink below the horizon into the waves of grass, the foal last disappearing as it brought up the rear, and then the horse that Lincomilla rode, inch by inch fade from sight, just as a ship slips down the round edge of the world. Her feet went first, then the *caronas* of her saddle, and by degrees her body, wrapped in the brown *chamál*.

"Lastly, the glory of her floating hair hung for a moment in his sight upon the sky, then vanished, just as a piece of seaweed is sucked into the tide by a receding wave.

"That's all," the story-teller said, and once again began to paint his horses' brands in the wood ashes with his mutton-bone, as he sat gazing at the fire.

Silence fell on the camp, and in the still, clear night the sound of the staked-out horses cropping the grass was almost a relief. None spoke, for nearly all had lost some kind of captive, in some way or other, till Claraz, rising, walked round and laid his hand upon the story-teller's shoulder. "I fear," he said, "the telling of the tale has not done anything to make the weight upon the heart any the lighter.

"All down the coast, as I remember, from Mazatlán to Acapulco, pearl-fishers used to say, unless a man made up his mind to stay below the water till his ears burst, that he would never be a first-rate pearl-diver.

"Some men could never summon up the courage, and remained indifferent pearl-divers, suffering great pain, and able to remain only a short time down in the depths, as their ears never burst. It seems to me that you are one of those . . . but, I know I am a fool, I like you better as you are."

He ceased, and the grey light of dawn fell on the sleepless camp on the north fork of the Mostazas (or perhaps the Naposta); it fell upon the smouldering fire, with Lincomilla's lover still drawing horses' marks in the damp ashes, and on the group of men wrapped in their ponchos shivering and restless with the first breath of day.

Out on the plain, some of the horses were lying down beside their bell-mares. Others stood hanging their heads low between their feet, with their coats ruffled by the dew.

A HUNDRED IN THE SHADE

THE river looked like a stream of oil flowing between the walls of dense, impenetrable woods that fringed its banks. Now and again it eddied strongly and seemed to boil, as some great rock or snag peeped up menacingly. Then it flowed on again resistlessly, bearing upon its yellow flood great trunks of Bongos or of Ceibas, as if they were but reeds. Toucans, looking as if they had been fashioned rather by Gian Baptista Porta than by nature, darted like king-fishers across its face. Parrots screeched harshly, and above the tallest trees, macaws, blue, red and orange, soared like hawks, looking as fitting to their natural surroundings as rooks in England cawing in the elms. Upon the sand-banks great saurians basked, and when they felt the passing steamer's wash, rolled into the stream, as noiselessly as water-rats in a canal.

Now and again a little clearing broke the hostile wall of the fierce-growing vegetation, with a few straw-thatched huts, a mango-tree or two, and a small patch of maize or yucca, with an unsubstantial fence of canes. Occasionally, where a stretch of plain intervened between the woods, a lean vaquero on a leaner horse, his hat blown back, forming a sort of aureole of straw behind his head, galloped along the banks after a point of steers, or merely raced the steamer for a few hundred yards and then, checking his horse, wheeled like a bird upon the wind. The steamer, painted a dazzling white, with decks piled one upon another till it looked like a floating house, belched out its thin wood smoke and panted as it fought the powerful, almost invisible current of the oily stream. Upon each side a barge was lashed, carrying a load of cattle that diminished day by day, as one was slaughtered every morning, in full sight of its doomed fellows, whose hooves were dyed red with the blood that flowed upon the deck.

As the boat forced its way up-stream the heat grew daily greater, and the fierce glare from the surface of the water more intense. The sun set in a dull, red orb, and from the banks there rose a thin, white mist. From the recesses of the forests came the cries of wild animals, silent by day, but roused into activity at night. The monkeys howled their full-throated chorus, jaguars and wild cats snarled, and in the stillness the brushwood rustled as some nocturnal animal passed through them stealthily. Clouds of mosquitoes filled the air, rendering sleep impossible. Even the freshness of the evening seemed to wear away as night wore on, and one by one the jaded passengers sought the topmost deck-house to try to catch the breeze.

Sprawling in wicker chairs, as the steamer forged along, the great black banks of vegetation sliding towards her as she passed, the passengers, mopping themselves and killing the mosquitoes now and then with a loud slap, relapsed into a moody silence, as they sipped iced drinks. Now and then someone cursed the heat, and now and then one or another of the perspiring band would walk to the thermometer, hung between the windows of the deck-house, and then exclaim, "Jesus! a hundred in the shade." One of the group of men who looked at him as a ship-wrecked sailor might look out for a sail, said, "In the moon, you mean," and sank back on his chair with as much elasticity as a sponge thrown out of a bath rebounds upon the floor.

At last, rounding a bend, a light breeze ruffled the surface of the river and brought a little life into the men lounging in their deck-chairs. No one could think of sleep in such conditions. Talk languished after a few general remarks about the price of cattle, and the usual stories about the prowess of the horses, the best in the whole world, that everyone had owned, for general conversation usually flags in a society of men, when women and horses have been discussed. No one spoke for a considerable time, as the steamer swept along through the dark alley of the woods, illuminated by a thousand million fire-flies flashing among the trees. The dark, blue southern sky, and the yellow waters of the stream, lighted up by the powerful port and starboard lights, appeared to frame the vessel in, and cut her off from all the world.

Without preamble, the orchid hunter, a thin, sunburned man, spectacled and bald, took up his parable. He told of having camped alone in Singapore, and being bitten on the forefinger of his left hand by some poisonous snake or other. "I had no antidote of any kind with me. My whisky bottle was quite empty. Not that I think it would have done much good had it been full, for I was so well soaked in it, I should have been obliged to drink a quart before it took effect on me. Yes, well, we orchid hunters as a rule are not teetotallers. Perhaps the damp, the solitude, or God knows what, soon drives most of us to drink. What did I do? Oh, yes, I sawed the finger off with a jack-knife. Of course it hurt; but it was just root hog or die. The worst of it is that the mosquitoes always fasten on the stump." He held up a brown mutilated hand for us to look at and then, after a long pull at his iced drink, sank back again into the silence that had become a second nature to him. Perhaps to those who practise orchid hunting it seems indecent to be talking, in the primeval silence of the woods.

To the disjointed story of the orchid hunter, that seemed to be extracted from him almost against his will, succeeded the impresario of a travelling operetta company, fluent and full of New York slang and jokes designed to please the intelligence of infant cavemen, long before wit or humour humanised the world. Withal not a bad fellow, for a man whose company, by his own confession, was half a brothel, and as difficult to drive as a whole waggon load of apes. A ranch man brought a whiff of purer air into the symposium, and as he sat tapping his leg with an imaginary whip, his thumb turned upwards from constant using of the lasso, his soft and soothing Western voice acted as a soporific on the company. They listened half awake to a long tale about the prowess of a Flathead Indian horse, "a buck-skin and a single footer, why, that yer hoice would pick a animal out of a bunch of steers, he knowed a fat one, too, better than a human, sure he did, that little hoice."

To him succeeded a traveller in a patent medicine that would cure snakebites, shingles, coughs, colds, and rheumatism. "What about earthquakes?" ejaculated someone. "Well, my stuff doesn't lay out to stop 'em; but it does no harm to 'em, anyway, and maybe might do some good to the survivors if they took it soon enough." He told us that he had never taken it himself, preferring good, sound whisky, but added, "I am its prophet, anyhow. 'One God, one Zamolina,' as good a creed as any other as far as I can see, and one a man can hold without much danger to his conscience, as long as the stuff sells."

The laugh that greeted the exposition of the creed of the patent medicine philosopher died away, and it appeared the experiences of the company had been exhausted. Confession, no matter if auricular or *coram publico*, generally extorts confession. Seated in the shade, so that up to the moment of his speaking no one had observed him, there was a quiet man, dressed in immaculate white clothes. His hundred dollar jipi-japa hat lay beside him on the deck. Somewhere about fifty years of age, his thick, dark hair was just beginning to turn grey. Tall and athletic looking, he still had not the look of being used to frontier life, and his quiet voice and manner showed him to have received what for the want of any better word is styled education, a thing that though it can do nothing to improve the faculties, yet now and then gives them the power of self-expression, in natures previously dumb.

"I don't know why I should tell you or anybody," he said, "this tale, experience or what you like to call it, except that as it happened to me twenty years ago to-day, it seems impersonal and as if it had occurred to some one I had known. I was young then." He paused and drew himself up a little, as a well-preserved man of fifty does when he refers to himself as old, all the time feeling women still turn round to look at him as he passes on the street. "I was young then. . . . It was in New Orleans that I met her, an English girl, living alone, *faisant la cocotte* as they say down there. I think it was in the St. Charles Hotel that I first saw her. Tall and red-haired, not too fat, not too thin, as the Arabs say when speaking of a handsome woman. What her real name was I never knew. I liked her far too well ever to wish to pry into her life. Her *nom de guerre* was Daphne Villiers, and by that name I knew and by degrees began to love her. She lived in one of those old streets that run into Lafayette Square, in the French quarter of the town. I forgot to say she spoke all languages, French, Spanish and Italian, German, and God knows what, indifferently well. A rare thing for an English-woman, even of her profession.

"Her rooms were furnished, not in the style you might expect, big looking-glasses, Louis Quinze chairs and tables, with reproductions of the Bath of Psyche, Venus and Cupid, French prints of women bathing, as Les Biches à la Mer, or La Puce, showing a girl of ample charms catching a flea upon her leg, but simply and in good taste. Two or three bits of china, good but inexpensive, with one fine piece of Ming, and a Rhodes plate or two were dotted here and there. Upon the walls were a few engravings of French pictures, with one or two water-colours and a pastel of herself, done, as she said, in Paris by a well-known pastelist, with the signature carefully erased. What struck me most about the rooms was a small cabinet of books. Anatole France and Guy de Maupassant, some poetry, with Adah Mencken's verses, and some manuals on china and on furniture, with Manon Lescaut, Dante's *Vita Nuova* and the *Heptameron* are what I recollect.

"There was a piano that she said 'of course is necessary in the métier,' on which she played not very well and sang French Creole songs with rather a good voice. Not having much to do at that time, I got to dropping in upon her whenever she was not engaged, not so much as a lover, but to enjoy a talk with someone whose mind did not entirely run upon the price of cotton, the sale of real estate, railway shares, dividends, the things in fact that citizens of God's Own Country chiefly converse about to the exclusion of all else. Curiously enough I was never jealous, although she often had to postpone my visits on account of her work. Of course, after the fashion of most women of her class, she always talked about 'my work.' She said she never drank except when she was working and I rather think that the use of the word kept me from being jealous, for I flattered myself she never used it when speaking of my visits to her.

"Little by little we grew almost indispensable to one another. I lent her books and literary magazines. How well I recollect bringing her *L'Imitation de Jésus* and how she laughed saying she knew it all by heart. 'Twas only then I found out that she was a Catholic; not that she cared too much for her religion, but as she said, the Mass with all there is about it, lights, incense and the tradition of antiquity, appealed to her on the æsthetic side. Yes, well, yes, I got to love her, and to look forward to our long talks on books and china, pictures and the like. I never took her out to theatres, for she said people would think that she was 'working' if they saw me with her, and she looked upon me as a friend. I like to hear her say so, for as time went on we had become quite as much friends as lovers, and I used to tell her everything that had happened to me since my last visit to her.

"She on her part used to advise me, as all women will advise the man they love. Though their advice may not be very weighty, yet a man is a fool who does not profit by it. One evening I went to see her, taking a big bunch of flowers, and when she thanked me I said, 'Congratulate me too, this is my birthday.' To my surprise she burst out crying, and for a long time I could not make her tell me the reason of her tears. At last she said, 'I should have liked to give you something, but you know how I live and I am sure you will not take a present from me.' Nothing that I could say would pacify her, although I swore that I would value anything she gave. For a long time she sobbed convulsively, till at last, drying her tears up with a handkerchief, she smiled and coming up to me, threw her arms round my neck and said, 'I have one thing that I can give you, that belongs entirely to me, that is myself.'

"Business kept me from seeing her again for several days. The more I thought about her, the more certain it appeared I could not live without her. So on the first opportunity I sought the curious old winding street in the French quarter of the town. The house looked strangely silent, and after knocking at the door for a long time the coloured girl I knew so well opened it, crying, holding a letter and a little packet in her hand. 'Missy Daphne, she done gone away,' she said, and looked at me reproachfully, as I thought afterwards. The letter told me she had gone off to Tampico with a mining engineer, not a bad fellow, who she thought would marry her. She said she had acted for the best, for both of us, and asked me to accept the little piece of Chinese pottery I so often had admired."

The story-teller ceased his tale just as a bird stops singing, when you expect he will go on. Silence fell on the hearers. It may be some of them had had presents on their birthdays, of less value than the teller's of the tale. No one said anything except the ranch man with the directness of a simple soul, "Reckon you missed the round-up that time, friend." The story-teller nodded at him, and walking up to the thermometer, muttered, "A hundred in the shade."

BEATTOCK FOR MOFFAT

THE bustle on the Euston platform stopped for an instant to let the men who carried him to the third-class compartment pass along the train. Gaunt and emaciated, he looked just at death's door, and, as they propped him in the carriage between two pillows, he faintly said: "Jock, do ye think I'll live as far as Moffat? I should na' like to die in London in the smoke."

His cockney wife, drying her tears with a cheap hem-stitched pocket handkerchief, her scanty town-bred hair looking like wisps of tow beneath her hat, bought from some window in which each individual article was marked at seven-and-sixpence, could only sob. His brother, with the country sun and wind burn still upon his face, and his huge hands hanging like hams in front of him, made answer.

"Andra'," he said, "gin ye last as far as Beattock, we'll gie ye a braw hurl back to the farm, syne the bask air, ye ken, and the milk, and, and—but can ye last as far as Beattock, Andra'?"

The sick man, sitting with the cold sweat upon his face, his shrunken limbs looking like sticks inside his ill-made black slop suit, after considering the proposition on its merits, looked up, and said: "I should na' like to bet I feel fair boss, God knows; but there, the mischief of it is, he will na' tell ye, so that, as ye may say, his knowlidge has na commercial value. I ken I look as gash as Garscadden. Ye mind, Jock, in the braw auld times, when the auld laird just slipped awa', whiles they were birlin' at the clairet. A braw death, Jock . . . do ye think it'll be rainin' aboot Ecclefechan? Aye . . . sure to be rainin' aboot Lockerbie. Nae Christians there, Jock, a' Johnstones and Jardines, ye mind?"

The wife, who had been occupied with an air cushion,

and, having lost the bellows, had been blowing into it till her cheeks seemed almost bursting, and her false teeth were loosened in her head, left off her toil to ask her husband "If 'e could pick a bit of something, a porkpie, or a nice sausage roll, or something tasty," which she could fetch from the refreshment room. The invalid having declined to eat, and his brother having drawn from his pocket a dirty bag, in which were peppermints, gave him a "drop," telling him that he "minded he aye used to like them weel, when the meenister had fairly got into his prelection in the auld kirk, outby."

The train slid almost imperceptibly away, the passengers upon the platform looking after it with that half-foolish, half-astonished look with which men watch a disappearing train. Then a few sandwich papers rose with the dust almost to the level of the platform, sank again, the clock struck twelve, and the station fell into a half quiescence, like a volcano in the interval between the lava showers. Inside the third-class carriage all was quiet until the lights of Harrow shone upon the left, when the sick man, turning himself with difficulty, said: "Good-bye, Harrow-on-the-Hill. I aye liked Harrow for the hill's sake, tho' ye can scarcely ca' yon wee bit mound a hill, Jean."

His wife, who, even in her grief, still smarted under the Scotch variant of her name, which all her life she had pronounced as "Jayne," and who, true cockney as she was, bounded her world within the lines of Plaistow, Peckham Rye, the Welsh 'Arp ('Endon way), and Willesden, moved uncomfortably at the depreciation of the chief mountain in her cosmos, but held her peace. Loving her husband in a sort of half-antagonistic fashion, born of the difference of type between the hard, unyielding, yet humorous and sentimental Lowland Scot, and the conglomerate of all races of the island which meet in London, and produce the weedy, shallow breed, almost incapable of reproduction, and yet high-strung and nervous, there had arisen between them that intangible veil of misconception which, though not excluding love, is yet impervious to respect. Each saw the other's failings, or, perhaps, thought the good qualities which each possessed were faults, for usually men judge each other by their good points, which, seen through prejudice of race, religion, and surroundings, appear to them defects.

The brother, who but a week ago had left his farm unwillingly, just when the "neeps were wantin' heughin' and a feck of' things requirin' to be done, forby a puckle sheep waitin' for keelin'," to come and see his brother for the last time, sat in that dour and seeming apathetic attitude which falls upon the country man, torn from his daily toil, and plunged into a town. Most things in London, during the brief intervals he had passed away from the sick-bed, seemed foolish to him, and of a nature such as a self-respecting Moffat man, in the hebdomadal enjoyment of the "prelections" of a Free Church minister could not authorise.

"Man, saw ye e'er a carter sittin' on his cart, and drivin' at a trot, instead o' walkin' in a proper manner alongside his horse?" had been his first remark.

The short-tailed sheep dogs, and the way they worked, the inferior quality of the cart-horses, their shoes with hardly any calkins worth the name, all was repugnant to him.

On Sabbath, too, he had received a shock, for, after walking miles to sit under the "brither of the U.P. minister at Symington," he had found Erastian hymn books in the pews, and noticed with stern reprobation that the congregation stood to sing, and that, instead of sitting solidly whilst the "man wrastled in prayer," stooped forward in the fashion called the Nonconformist lounge.

His troubled spirit had received refreshment from the sermon, which, though short, and extending to but some five-and-forty minutes, had still been powerful, for he said:

"When yon wee, shilpit meenister—brither, ye ken, of rantin' Ferguson, out by Symington—shook the congregation ower the pit mouth, ye could hae fancied that the very

68

sowls in hell just girned. Man, he garred the very stour to flee aboot the kirk, and, hadna' the big book been weel brass-banded, he would hae dang the haricles fair oot."

So the train slipped past Watford, swaying round the curves like a gigantic serpent, and jolting at the facing points as a horse "pecks" in his gallop at an obstruction in the ground.

The moon shone brightly into the compartment, extinguishing the flickering of the half-candle power electric light. Rugby, the station all lit up, and with its platforms occupied but by a few belated passengers, all muffled up like race-horses taking their exercise, flashed past. They slipped through Cannock Chase, which stretches down with heath and firs, clear brawling streams, and birch trees, an outpost of the north lost in the midland clay. They crossed the oily Trent, flowing through alder copses, and with its backwaters all overgrown with lilies, like an aguapey in Paraguay or in Brazil.

The sick man, wrapped in cheap rugs, and sitting like Guy Fawkes, in the half-comic, half-pathetic way that sick folk sit, making them sport for fools, and, at the same time, moistening the eye of the judicious, who reflect that they themselves may one day sit as they do, bereft of all the dignity of strength, looked listlessly at nothing as the train sped on. His loving, tactless wife, whose cheap "sized" handkerchief had long since become a rag with mopping up her tears, endeavoured to bring round her husband's thoughts to paradise, which she conceived a sort of music hall, where angels sat with their wings folded, listening to sentimental songs.

Her brother-in-law, reared on the fiery faith of Moffat Calvinism, eyed her with great disfavour, as a terrier eyes a rat imprisoned in a cage.

"Jean wumman," he burst out, "to hear ye talk, I would jist think your meenister had been a perfectly illeeterate man, pairadise here, pairadise there, what do ye think a man like Andra' could dae daunderin' aboot a gairden naked, pu'in' soor aipples frae the trees?"

Cockney and Scotch conceit, impervious alike to outside criticism, and each so bolstered in its pride as to be quite incapable of seeing that anything existed outside the purlieus of their sight, would soon have made the carriage into a battlefield, had not the husband, with the authority of approaching death, put in his word.

"Whist, Jeanie wumman. Jock, dae ye no ken that the Odium-Theologicum is just a curse—pairadise—set ye baith up—pairadise. I dinna' even richtly ken if I can last as far as Beattock."

Stafford, its iron furnaces belching out flames, which burned red holes into the night, seemed to approach, rather than be approached, so smoothly ran the train. The mingled moonlight and the glare of iron-works lit the canal beside the railway, and from the water rose white vapours as from Styx or Periphlegethon. Through Cheshire ran the train, its timbered houses showing ghastly in the frost which coated all the carriage windows, and rendered them opaque. Preston, the Catholic city, lay silent in the night, its river babbling through the public park, and then the hills of Lancashire loomed lofty in the night. Past Garstang, with its water-lily-covered ponds, Garstang where, in the days gone by, Catholic squires, against their will, were forced on Sundays to "take wine" in Church on pain of fine, the puffing serpent slid.

The talk inside the carriage had given place to sleep, that is, the brother-in-law and wife slept fitfully, but the sick man looked out, counting the miles to Moffat, and speculating on his strength. Big drops of sweat stood on his forehead, and his breath came double, whistling through his lungs.

They passed by Lancaster, skirting the sea on which the moon shone bright, setting the fishing boats in silver as they lay scarcely moving on the waves. Then, so to speak, the train set its face up against Shap Fell, and, puffing heavily, drew up into the hills, the scattered grey stone houses of the north, flanked by their gnarled and twisted ash trees, hanging upon the edge of the streams, as lonely, and as cut off from the world (except the passing train) as they had been in Central Africa. The moorland roads, winding amongst the heather, showed that the feet of generations had marked them out, and not the line, spade, and theodolite, with all the circumstance of modern road makers. They, too, looked white and unearthly in the moonlight, and now and then a sheep, aroused by the snorting of the train, moved from the heather into the middle of the road, and stood there motionless, its shadow filling the narrow track, and flickering on the heather at the edge.

The keen and penetrating air of the hills and night roused the two sleepers, and they began to talk, after the Scottish fashion, of the funeral, before the anticipated corpse.

"Ye ken, we've got a braw new hearse outby, sort of Epescopalian lookin', we' gless a' roond, so's ye can see the kist. Very conceity too, they mak' the hearses noo-a-days. I min' when they were jist auld sort o' ruckly boxes, awfu' licht, ye ken, upon the springs, and just went dodderin' alang, the body swingin' to and fro, as if it would flee richt oot. The roads, ye ken, were no high hand so richtly metalled in thae days."

The subject of the conversation took it cheerfully, expressing pleasure at the advance of progress as typefied in the new hearse, hoping his brother had a decent "stan' o' black," and looking at his death, after the fashion of his kind, as it were something outside himself, a fact indeed, on which, at the same time, he could express himself with confidence as being in some measure interested. His wife, not being Scotch, took quite another view, and seemed to think that the mere mention of the word was impious, or, at the least, of such a nature as to bring on immediate dissolution, holding the English theory that unpleasant things should not be mentioned, and that, by this means, they can be kept at bay. Half from affection, half from the inborn love of cant, inseparable from the true Anglo-Saxon, she

endeavoured to persuade her husband that he looked better,
and yet would mend, once in his native air.

"At Moffit, ye'd 'ave the benefit of the 'ill breezes, and that
'ere country milk, which never 'as no cream in it, but 'ole-
some, as you say. Why yuss, in about eight days at Moffit,
you'll be as 'earty as you ever was. Yuss, you will, you take
my word."

Like a true Londoner, she did not talk religion, being too
thin in mind and body even to have grasped the dogma of the
sects. Her Heaven a music 'all, her paradise to see the king
drive through the streets, her literary pleasure to read lies in
newspapers, or pore on novelettes, which showed her the
pure elevated lives of duchesses, placing the knaves and
prostitutes within the limits of her own class; which view of
life she accepted as quite natural, and as a thing ordained to
be by the bright stars who write.

Just at the Summit they stopped an instant to let a goods
train pass, and, in a faint voice, the consumptive said: "I'd
almost lay a wager now I'd last to Moffat, Jock. The Shap, ye
ken, I aye looked at as the beginning of the run home. The
hills, ye ken, are sort o' heartsome. No that they're bonny
hills like Moffat hills, na', na', ill-shapen sort of things, just
like Borunty tatties, awfu' puir names too, Shap Fell and
Rowland Edge, Hutton Roof Crags, and Arnside Fell; heard
ever ony body sich like names for hills? Naething to fill the
mooth; man, the Scotch hills jist grap ye in the mooth for a'
the world like speerits."

They stopped at Penrith, which the old castle walls make
even meaner, in the cold morning light, than other stations
look. Little Salkeld, and Armathwaite, Cotehill, and Scotby
all rushed past, and the train, slackening, stopped with a jerk
upon the platform, at Carlisle. The sleepy porters bawled out
"change for Maryport," some drovers slouched into carriages,
kicking their dogs before them, and, slamming-to the doors,
exchanged the time of day with others of their tribe, all
carrying ash or hazel sticks, all red-faced and keen-eyed, their

caps all crumpled, and their greatcoat-tails all creased, as if their wearers had lain down to sleep full dressed, so as to lose no time in getting to the labours of the day. The old red sandstone church, with something of a castle in its look, as well befits a shrine close to a frontier where in days gone by the priest had need to watch and pray, frowned on the passing train, and on the manufactories, whose banked-up fires sent poisonous fumes into the air, withering the trees which, in the public park, a careful council had hedged round about with wire.

The Eden ran from bank to bank, its water swirling past as wildly as when "The Bauld Buccleugh" and his Moss Troopers, bearing "the Kinmount" fettered in their midst, plunged in and passed it, whilst the keen Lord Scroope stood on the brink amazed and motionless. Gretna, so close to England, and yet a thousand miles away in speech and feeling, found the sands now flying through the glass. All through the mosses which once were the "Debatable Land" on which the moss-troopers of the clan Graeme were used to hide the cattle stolen from the "auncient enemy," the now repatriated Scotchman murmured feebly "that it was bonny scenery" although a drearier prospect of "moss hags" and stunted birch trees is not to be found. At Ecclefechan he just raised his head, and faintly spoke of "yon auld carle, Carlyle, ye ken, a dour thrawn body, but a gran' pheelosopher," and then lapsed into silence, broken by frequent struggles to take breath.

His wife and brother sat still, and eyed him as a cow watches a locomotive engine pass, amazed and helpless, and he himself had but the strength to whisper: "Jock, I'm dune, I'll no' see Moffat, blast it, yon smoke, ye ken, yon London smoke has been ower muckle for ma lungs."

The tearful, helpless wife, not able even to pump up the harmful and unnecessary conventional lie, which after all consoles only the liar, sat pale and limp, chewing the fingers of her Berlin gloves. Upon the weather-beaten cheek of Jock glistened a tear, which he brushed off as angrily as it had been a wasp.

"Aye, Andra'," he said, "I would hae liket awfu' weel that ye should win to Moffat. Man, the rowan trees are a' in bloom, and there's a bonny breer upon the corn—aye, ou aye, the reid bogs are lookin' gran' the year—but Andra', I'll tak' ye east to the auld kirk yaird, ye'll na' ken onything aboot it, but we'll hae a heartsome funeral."

Lockerbie seemed to fly towards them, and the dying Andra' smiled as his brother pointed out the place and said: "Ye mind, there are na' ony Christians in it" and answered: "Aye, I mind, naething but Jardines," as he fought for breath.

The death dews gathered on his forehead as the train shot by Nethercleugh, passed Wamphray, and Dinwoodie, and with a jerk pulled up at Beattock just at the summit of the pass.

So in the cold spring morning light, the fine rain beating on the platform, as the wife and brother got their almost speechless care out of the carriage, the brother whispered: "Dam't, ye've done it, Andra', here's Beattock; I'll tak' ye east to Moffat yet to dee."

But on the platform, huddled on the bench to which he had been brought, Andra' sat speechless and dying in the rain. The doors banged to, the guard stepping in lightly as the train flew past, and a belated porter shouted, "Beattock, Beattock for Moffat," and then, summoning his last strength, Andra' smiled, and whispered faintly in his brother's ear: "Aye, Beattock—for Moffat?" Then his head fell back, and a faint bloody foam oozed from his pallid lips. His wife stood crying helplessly, the rain beating upon the flowers of her cheap hat, rendering it shapeless and ridiculous. But Jock, drawing out a bottle, took a short dram and saying, "Andra', man, ye made a richt gude fecht o' it," snorted an instant in a red pocket handkerchief, and calling up a boy, said: "Rin, Jamie, to the toon, and tell McNicol to send up and fetch a corp." Then, after helping to remove the body to the waiting-room, walked out into the rain, and, whistling "Corn Rigs" quietly between his teeth lit up his pipe, and muttered as he smoked: "A richt gude fecht—man aye, ou aye, a game yin Andra', puir felly. Weel, weel, he'll hae a braw hurl onyway in the new Moffat hearse."

AT NAVALCAN

WE had been riding through the open park-like oak forests that had been sown with corn, now reaped, at the fast jog known as the Castilian pace. It had not rained for months, and the rough trail lay inches deep in dust as white as flour. The greyhounds following us lolled out their tongues like long, red rags, and trotted on resignedly close to the horses' heels. Not a bird stirred in the torrid heat. The air seemed as if heated in a furnace, and a few cattle here and there stood motionless in the dry streams, as if they knew that there was water underneath the surface, although they could not reach it. The bark upon the cork-trees scattered among the oaks seemed bursting. Even the lizards appeared to run across the track as if they did so under protest, scared by our horses' feet.

Nicolás checked his lean, roan mare, and stopping in a long account of his adventures in the Manigua of Cuba, where in days past he had served against Maximo Gomez and Maceo, pointing to a conglomeration of brown, dusty houses that clustered round the tower of a church, a mile or two away, said: "There is Navalcán. They will be dancing in the plaza already, Don Roberto," he said; "let us push on and see them in their old dresses, for in Navalcán they are still Spaniards as God made them in days past. Old Cirilo's daughter was married this morning, and we shall be in time to see the fiesta if we spur a bit."

He settled himself back upon his saddle, and with his face tanned by the tropics and his native sun, his suit of dark grey velveteen, and his short jacket, over which he wore a leather shoulder-belt with a great boss of brass stamped with the arms of the Dukes of Frias, for he was their head gamekeeper, he looked just like the yeoman on the good grey mare that he was riding "a la gineta" who Cervantes has immortalised.

We spurred our horses, passed by the ruined Roman bridge with its high arch spanning the dried-up river, stopped for a moment under a gnarled oak-tree, for Nicolás to point out where he had killed a wolf last winter, and diving down a steep path like the bed of a torrent, entered the outskirts of the old-world town. Men upon donkeys and on mules, with now and then a horseman sitting high on his semi-Moorish saddle, his feet encased in iron shoe stirrups, passed us, all going to the feast. Pigs ran about the streets, as much at home as Peter in his house, as Nicolás observed. Children, ragged, bright-eyed and dirty, stared at the passers-by from the doors of houses, as Kaffir children might stare at a strange white man passing before their kraal.

We clattered up a steep and stony lane, the horses' shoes striking a stream of sparks from the rough stones, and got off at the house of one Cirilo, an ex-alcalde of the town. Short, stout, dressed in black velveteen, a broad black sash wound three or four times about his waist, a stiff and broad-brimmed black felt hat upon his head and alpargatas on his feet, he seemed descended apostolically from Sancho Panza, both in appearance and in speech. Our horses were led by one of Cirilo's sons, just in the way Cervantes describes, when the Knight of the Rueful Figure and his squire arrived at many another such a little town as Navalcán. Assembled in the chief room of the house, adorned with a few pictures of the saints, a curious piece of old embroidery in a black frame, and several trophies of the chase, were all the notabilities. Much did we salute each other, inquiring minutely after the state of health of all our separate families, and being assured that the poor house in which we sat was ours. The mistress of the place and her two tall daughters stood about, talking and bringing wine, lemonade, and cakes of meal and honey, with the same white, flake pastry that the Moors left in Spain and that is to be seen to-day in every house in Fez and Tetuán.

They stood about, sitting down only occasionally and as if under protest, for in old-world places such as Navalcán, women, all unknown to themselves, have still continued the old Arab custom of never sitting down to eat together with the men. Being strangers in that remote and time-neglected village, we also in a way acted as newspapers. "What of Morocco and the accursed war? Neighbour Remigio has a son there fighting the infidel. He cannot use the pen, so that his father does not know if he is alive or dead." Then with a touch of that materialistic scepticism that is at once the strength and weakness of the race: "The big fish make their harvest out of it, I suppose, for, in disturbed rivers fishermen find their gain." Cirilo took off his hat and wiped his forehead, conscious that by the enunciation of a proverb he had clinched the matter for all time. Our hats he had begged us to take off, and placed them on a chair, for a guest's hat in old-world towns in Spain is handled with respect.

The conversation ran a good deal on the price of pigs, of mules, sheep, horses and other matters that men of culture take their delight in talking of the whole world over. All governments were bad, and politics the ruin of a country, yet none of them ever in his life lifted a hand to change a government, but talked of politics for hours. The clergy too were rogues who did no work of any kind, were drones and cumberers of the earth, yet they went religiously to mass, and when the parish priest came round to drink a glass of wine with us, all rose up courteously to do him reverence. A native of Asturias, a province he described as quite a paradise, the priest gave it as his opinion that England was by degrees emancipating herself from the bonds of the heresy that Henry VIII and his accursed concubine, Ana Bolena, had promulgated. I said I thought it might be so, and that when all was said and done Ana Bolena had paid dearly, both for her carnal lapses and her heresy. As one who is enunciating an eternal verity, Father Camacho rejoined in a grave voice: "Sir, she is burning in hell fire for all eternity." I left it at that, hoping the faggots might be after all made of asbestos and the poor sinner's sufferings mitigated by the intervention of Jehovah's other self, Allah, the Merciful, the Compassionate.

After a round of the strong, harsh, red wine that in those parts is jocularly referred to as "Peleón," that is, the fighter, whether from its effect upon the stomach or the brain is doubtful, washed down with sweet and sticky lemonade, Cirilo said the dancing in the plaza had begun. The ceremony in the church had taken place at eleven in the morning, so that the happy pair were actually joined in holy matrimony, or as the country people say, "married in Latin," and in their new estate were welcoming their friends.

Outside the door the strains of the dulzaina, the Arab pipe the Moors left in Spain, accompanied by the sacramental drum, mixed with the blare of a brass band. The little winding streets were like the beds of torrents, with great live rocks coming to the surface, worn smooth and slippery by the passing feet of mules and horses since Navalcán was Navalcán. Men passed who might have stepped out of past centuries, all in the old Castilian peasant's dress, made of black velveteen, short jackets, open waistcoats and frilled shirts. They wore black broad-brimmed hats over silk handkerchiefs bound round their heads with the ends hanging down like tails. Where the streets were free from rocks the white dust lay so thickly that the feet of the passers-by, all shod with alpargatas, made no more sound than if it had been snow on which they walked. Now and again, above the music of the band, came a wild cry from one of the excited village youths, so like the neighing of a horse it seemed impossible that it was not a stallion calling to a mare.

A mass of country people filled the middle of the square. Only one man, a neighbouring proprietor, was dressed in modern clothes. The women, for the most part, wore gay-coloured petticoats, giving them a look of humming tops as they moved to and fro. Over their skirts they had a long lace apron, worked in elaborate openwork designs, that in most cases had been generations in their families. Under their short basque jackets their loose white blouses, elaborately worked and frilled, swelled out like pouter pigeons' crops. Their heads were bare, and their thick hair, as black as jet, was parted in the middle, brushed close against their cheeks, and plaited into two long pigtails, hanging down their backs. All wore gold earrings worked in filigree, and round their necks strings of gold beads, heirlooms from older days. Their feet were shod with dark, brown leather shoes, latched on the instep and cut in open patterns by a rustic shoemaker. Though they were peasants they all walked with the incomparable carriage of the women of their race, with the slight motion of the hips that sets the petticoats a-swinging, just as a horse's tail swings very gently to and fro at the Castilian pace.

The dancers formed a long line down the middle of the square, the men and women standing opposite each other. The bride and bridegroom stood in the middle of the line. The bride, tall, handsome, dark and active on her feet as a wild colt, wore a silk skirt almost concealed under the folds of old-fashioned coarse lace that had belonged to her great-grandmother. Upon her head she wore the "Cresta," a high knot of ribbon shaped something like a coxcomb, to show she had never made a slip of any kind. This badge, the people said, was getting rarer than it used to be for brides, a circumstance that they attributed to the decay of morals, that had been going on continuously for the last five hundred years. This bride upheld the ancient purity of Castilian morals in spite of being five-and-twenty years of age. It somehow made one think about the girl who had received the prize of virtue five years running, and in the comic opera remarked: "Oui, cinq fois rosière, c'est joli, mais cristi! que c'est dur."

The bridegroom, a tall, swarthy youth, who had already

an anticipatory air of cuckledom about him, between excitement and the wine that he had evidently drunk was streaming down with sweat. Still, when the band, placed just beneath the village cross, struck up a lively Jota he capered nimbly, first with one girl, then with another, snapping his fingers like a pair of castagnettes, with his arms held above his shoulders and waving to and fro. A thick, white dust covered the dancers' old-fashioned dresses, as it were with flour, and falling on the women's black and glossy hair, gave it a look of being powdered, not unbecoming to them.

When the band stopped from sheer exhaustion and the dulzaina players' cheeks were for a spell deflated, great pitchers of rough earthenware full of the heady country wine were handed round among the crowd. They drank, first looking towards the bride, and wishing her long life and many children, then drew the backs of their brown, toil-stained hands across their mouths, tightened their sashes, and after taking one of the black and coarsely made cigars the bridegroom went about offering to everybody from a brown paper parcel, fell to a-dancing, with the cigars behind their ears. Wild goats or antelopes could not have been more active than the youths and maidens; the swing and perseverance of the band were wonderful. The elders stood about in groups, smoking the rank, ill-made cigars that a paternal Government in Spain provides at its own prices to its citizens.

The band ceased suddenly, without a warning, just as a gipsy song ends, on a long-drawn-out note. The men, after their fashion of the kind the whole world over, collected into groups and criticised the girls as they walked to and fro with their arms round each other's waists. Great tables were laid out in the patio of a house, with rows of pitchers filled with wine and round hard rolls upon the spotless tablecloth, making one think of Leonardo's "Last Supper," and hope no Judas would intrude upon the feast. In the house where the happy pair were going to reside their friends and neighbours all had brought their offerings. Jugs, pots, pans, washing-basins, hoes, spades and axes, great skins of wine, salt, sugar, coffee; innumerable bundles of cigars, adzes and planes, saws, gimlets, and almost every article of rural life lay piled upon the floor. A load of wood, sacks of potatoes, with jars of olives and of oil, recalled a wedding such as Theocritus might have celebrated.

Then, entering the house, the bride received us, and all the strangers, who had not come provided with their household offerings, presented five or ten dollars to the bridegroom, who thanked them fluently in such well-chosen language as few dwellers in the north, men of much more education than himself, could hope to compass. He handed all the money to the bride, who put it carefully into a bag she carried by her side and thanked the givers, who once again wished her health and happiness, with many children and long-drawn-out years, with self-possession and the grave air of dignity that comes so naturally to the Castilians. Cirilo hoped that she would imitate her mother, who had thirteen children, and his daughter, smiling at him, rejoined that she would try.

In an inside apartment, that in Spain is called an alcove, without a window and stiflingly hot, was placed the marriage bed. Full five feet from the ground it stood, with mattress upon mattress piled mountains high, a great lace valence worked by the bride herself in antique patterns of men on horseback, tall cypresses, and crosses here and there, swept down and touched the floor. The coverlet was lace, made by the mother of the bride and by her sisters, and the four curtains hanging from the posts were of a curious kind of needlework, exactly like that made by the Moorish women in North Africa. In a dark outhouse, outside the bridal chamber with its four-poster bed, were laid a plank or two, covered with several sheepskins and a rug. This Spartan couch tradition had provided for the bridegroom, who had to occupy it till the last guest retired.

Once more Cirilo took us to his house, and once again regaled us with wine and lemonade, cakes, coffee, and with old-world sweetmeats, made of the kernels of a pine-cone, stewed in honey, into a sticky little slab. We mounted at his door, with all his family holding the stirrups and the reins; wished him farewell with a cascade of thanks, and picked our way through the dark streets, our horses plunging wildly now and then, for from each door the citizens were sending rockets whizzing through the air, and serpents ran along the stones, exploding loudly and shedding a blue glare upon the ground.

Outside the town, when we had got a pull upon our horses, the moon had risen, making the bushes take fantastic shapes, and look like animals, ready to spring upon us. The mountains of the Gredos looked unearthly in the moonlight, the shrill cicalas kept up a continuous singing, and neither Nicolás nor I said anything for a mile or two, till turning round he asked me: "Have you seen anything like that in England, Don Roberto?" To which I answered: "No."

THE GOLD FISH

OUTSIDE the little straw-thatched café in a small courtyard trellised with vines, before a miniature table
painted in red and blue, and upon which stood a dome-
shaped pewter teapot and a painted glass half filled with mint,
sat Amarabat, resting and smoking hemp. He was of those
whom Allah in his mercy (or because man in the Blad-Allah
has made no railways) has ordained to run. Set upon the
road, his shoes pulled up, his waistband tightened, in his hand
a staff, a palm-leaf wallet at his back, and in it bread, some
hemp, a match or two (known to him as el spiritus), and a
letter to take anywhere, crossing the plains, fording the
streams, stuggling along the mountain-paths, sleeping but
fitfully, a burning rope steeped in saltpetre fastened to his
foot, he trotted day and night—untiring as a camel, faithful
as a dog. In Rabat as he sat dozing, watching the greenish
smoke curl upwards from his hemp pipe, word came to him
from the Khalifa of the town. So Amarabat rose, paid for his
tea with half a handful of defaced and greasy copper coins,
and took his way towards the white palace with the crenelated
walls, which on the cliff, hanging above the roaring tide-rip,
just inside the bar of the great river, looks at Salee. Around
the horseshoe archway of the gate stood soldiers, wild, fierce-
eyed, armed to the teeth, descendants, most of them, of the
famed warriors whom Sultan Muley Ismail (may God have
pardoned him!) bred for his service, after the fashion of the
Carlylean hero Frederic; and Amarabat walked through them,
not aggressively, but with the staring eyes of a confirmed
hemp-smoker, with the long stride of one who knows that
he is born to run, and the assurance of a man who waits upon
his lord. Sometime he waited whilst the Khalifa dispensed
what he thought justice, chaffered with Jewish pedlars for

cheap European goods, gossiped with friends, looked at the antics of a dwarf, or priced a Georgian or Circassian girl brought with more care than glass by some rich merchant from the East. At last Amarabat stood in the presence, and the Khalifa, sitting upon a pile of cushions, playing with a Waterbury watch, a pistol and a Koran by his side, addressed him thus:

"Amarabat, son of Bjorma, my purpose is to send thee to Tafilet, where our liege lord the Sultan lies with his camp. Look upon this glass bowl made by the Kaffir, but clear as is the crystal of the rock; see how the light falls on the water, and the shifting colours that it makes, as when the Bride of the Rain stands in the heavens, after a shower in spring. Inside are seven gold fish, each scale as bright as letters in an Indian book. The Christian from whom I bought them said originally they came from the Far East where the Djin-descended Jawi live, the little yellow people of the faith. That may be, but such as they are, they are a gift for kings. Therefore, take thou the bowl. Take it with care, and bear it as it were thy life. Stay not, but in an hour start from the town. Delay not on the road, be careful of the fish, change not their water at the muddy pool where tortoises bask in the sunshine, but at running brooks; talk not to friends, look not upon the face of woman by the way, although she were as a gazelle, or as the maiden who when she walked through the fields the sheep stopped feeding to admire. Stop not, but run through day and night, pass through the Atlas at the Glaui; beware of frost, cover the bowl with thine own haik; upon the other side shield me the bowl from the Saharan sun, and drink not of the water if thou pass a day athirst when toiling through the sand. Break not the bowl, and see the fish arrive in Tafilet, and then present them, with this letter, to our lord. Allah be with you, and his Prophet; go, and above all things see thou breakest not the bowl." And Amarabat, after the manner of his kind, taking the bowl of gold fish, placed one hand upon his heart and said: "Inshallah, it shall be as thou hast said. God gives the feet and lungs. He also gives the luck upon the road."

So he passed out under the horseshoe arch, holding the bowl almost at arms' length so as not to touch his legs, and with the palmetto string by which he carried it, bound round with rags. The soldiers looked at him, but spoke not, and their eyes seemed to see far away, and to pass over all in the middle distance, though no doubt they marked the smallest detail of his gait and dress. He passed between the horses of the guard all standing nodding under the fierce sun, the reins tied to the cantles of their high red saddles, a boy in charge of every two or three: he passed beside the camels resting by the well, the donkeys standing dejected by the firewood they had brought: passed women, veiled white figures going to the baths; and passing underneath the lofty gateway of the town, exchanged a greeting with the half-mad, half-religious beggar just outside the walls, and then emerged upon the sandy road, between the aloe hedges, which skirts along the sea. So as he walked, little by little he fell into his stride; then got his second wind, and smoking now and then a pipe of hemp, began, as Arabs say, to eat the miles, his eyes fixed on the horizon, his stick stuck down between his shirt and back, the knob protruding over the left shoulder like the hilt of a two-handed sword. And still he held the precious bowl from Franquestan in which the golden fish swam to and fro, diving and circling in the sunlight, or flapped their tails to steady themselves as the water danced with the motion of his steps. Never before in his experience had he been charged with such a mission, never before been sent to stand before Allah's vicegerent upon earth. But still the strangeness of his business was what preoccupied him most. The fish like molten gold, the water to be changed only at running streams the fish to be preserved from frost and sun; and then the bowl: had not the Khalifa said at the last, "Beware, break not the bowl"? So it appeared to him that most undoubtedly a charm was in the fish and in the bowl, for who sends common fish on such a journey through the land? Then he resolved at any hazard to bring them safe and keep the bowl intact, and trotting onward, smoked his hemp, and wondered why he of all men should have had the luck to bear the precious gift. He knew he kept his law, at least as far as a poor man can keep it, prayed when he thought of prayer, or was assailed by terror in the night alone upon the plains; fasted in Ramadan, although most of his life was one continual fast; drank of the shameful but seldom, and on the sly, so as to give offence to no believer, and seldom looked upon the face of the strange women, Daughters of the Illegitimate, whom Sidna Mohammed himself has said, avoid. But all these things he knew were done by many of the faithful, and so he did not set himself up as of exceeding virtue, but rather left the praise to God, who helped his slave with strength to keep his law. Then left off thinking, judging the matter was ordained, and trotted, trotted over the burning plains, the gold fish dancing in the water as the miles melted and passed away.

Duar and Kasbah, castles of the Caids, Arabs' black tents, suddra zaribas, camels grazing—antediluvian in appearance—on the little hills, the muddy streams edged all along the banks with oleanders, the solitary horsemen holding their long and brass-hooped guns, like spears, the white-robed noiseless-footed travellers on the roads, the chattering storks upon the village mosques, the cow-birds sitting on the cattle in the fields—he saw, but marked not, as he trotted on. Day faded into night, no twilight intervening, and the stars shone out, Soheil and Rigel with Betelgeuse and Aldebaran, and the three bright lamps which the cursed Christians know as the Three Maries—called, he supposed, after the mother of their Prophet; and still he trotted on. Then by the side of a lone palm-tree springing up from a cleft in a tall rock, an island on the plain, he stopped to pray; and sleeping, slept but fitfully, the strangeness of the business making him wonder; and he who cavils over matters in the night can never rest, for thus the jackal and the hyena pass their nights talking and reasoning about the thoughts which fill their minds when men die with their faces covered in their haiks, and after prayer sleep. Rising after an hour or two and going to the nearest stream, he changed the water of his fish, leaving a little in the bottom of the bowl, and dipping with his brass drinking-cup into the stream for fear of accidents. He passed the Kasbah of el Daudi, passed the land of the Rahamna, accursed folk always in "siba," saw the great snowy wall of Atlas rise, skirted Marakesh, the Kutubieh, rising first from the plain and sinking last from sight as he approached the mountains and left the great white city sleeping in the plain.

Little by little the country altered as he ran: cool streams for muddy rivers, groves of almond-trees, ashes and elms, with grape-vines binding them together as the liana binds the canela and the urunday in the dark forests of Brazil and Paraguay. At midday when the sun was at its height, when locusts, whirring through the air, sank in the dust as flying-fish sink in the waves, when palm-trees seem to nod their heads, and lizards are abroad drinking the heat and basking in the rays, when the dry air shimmers, and sparks appear to dance before the traveller's eye, and a thin, reddish dust lies on the leaves, on clothes of men, and upon every hair of horses' coats, he reached a spring. A river springing from a rock, or issuing after running underground, had formed a little pond. Around the edge grew bulrushes, great catmace, water-soldiers, tall arums and metallic-looking sedge-grass, which gave an air as of an outpost of the tropics lost in the desert sand. Fish played beneath the rock where the stream issued, flitting to and fro, or hanging suspended for an instant in the clear stream, darted into the dark recesses of the sides; and in the middle of the pond enormous tortoises, horrid and antediluvian-looking, basked with their backs awash or raised their heads to snap at flies, and all about them hung a dark and fetid slime.

A troop of thin brown Arab girls filled their tall amphoræ

whilst washing in the pond. Placing his bowl of fish upon a jutting rock, the messenger drew near. "Gazelles," he said, "will one of you give me fresh water for the Sultan's golden fish?" Laughing and giggling, the girls drew near, looked at the bowl, had never seen such fish. "Allah is great; why do you not let them go in the pond and play a little with their brothers?" And Amarabat with a shiver answered, "Play, let them play! and if they come not back my life will answer for it." Fear fell upon the girls, and one advancing, holding the skirt of her long shift between her teeth to veil her face, poured water from her amphora upon the fish.

Then Amarabat, setting down his precious bowl, drew from his wallet a pomegranate and began to eat, and for a farthing buying a piece of bread from the women, was satisfied, and after smoking, slept, and dreamed he was approaching Tafilet; he saw the palm-trees rising from the sand; the gardens; all the oasis stretching beyond his sight; at the edge the Sultan's camp, a town of canvas, with the horses, camels, and the mules picketed, all in rows, and in the midst of the great "duar" the Sultan's tent, like a great palace all of canvas, shining in the sun. All this he saw, and saw himself entering the camp, delivering up his fish, perhaps admitted to the sacred tent, or at least paid by a vizier as one who has performed his duty well. The slow match blistering his foot, he woke to find himself alone, the "gazelles" departed, and the sun shining on the bowl, making the fish appear more magical, more wondrous, brighter, and more golden than before.

And so he took his way along the winding Atlas paths, and slept at Demnats, then, entering the mountains, met long trains of travellers going to the south. Passing through groves of chestnuts, walnut-trees, and hedges thick with blackberries and travellers' joy, he climbed through vineyards rich with black Atlas grapes, and passed the flat mud-built Berber villages nestling against the rocks. Eagles flew by and moufflons gazed at him from the peaks, and from the thickets of lentiscus and dwarf arbutus wild boars appeared, grunted, and slowly walked across the path, and still he climbed, the icy wind from off the snow chilling him in his cotton shirt, for his warm Tadla haik was long ago wrapped round the bowl to shield the precious fish. Crossing the Wad Ghadat, the current to his chin, his bowl of fish held in one hand, he struggled on. The Berber tribesmen at Tetsula and Zarkten, hard-featured, shaved but for a chin-tuft, and robed in their "achnifs" with the curious eye woven in the skirt, saw he was a "rekass," or thought the fish not worth their notice, so gave him a free road. Night caught him at the stone-built, antediluvian-looking Kasbah of the Glaui, perched in the eye of the pass, with the small plain of Teluet two thousand feet below. Off the high snow-peaks came a whistling wind, water froze solid in all the pots and pans, earthenware jars and bottles throughout the castle, save in the bowl which Amarabat, shivering and miserable, wrapped in his haik and held close to the embers, hearing the muezzin at each call to prayers; praying himself to keep awake so that his fish might live. Dawn saw him on the trail, the bowl wrapped in a woollen rag, and the fish fed with bread-crumbs, but himself hungry and his head swimming with want of sleep, with smoking "kief," and with the bitter wind which from El Tisi N'Glaui flagellates the road. Right through the valley of Teluet he still kept on, and day and night still trotting, trotting on, changing his bowl almost instinctively from hand to hand, a broad leaf floating on the top to keep the water still, he left Agurzga, with its twin castles, Ghresat and Dads, behind. Then rapidly descending, in a day reached an oasis between Todghra and Ferkla, and rested at a village for the night. Sheltered by palm-trees and hedged round with cactuses and aloes, either to keep out thieves or as a symbol of the thorniness of life, the village lay, looking back on the white Atlas gaunt and mysterious, and on the other side towards the brown Sahara, land of the palm-tree (Belad-el-Jerid), the refuge of the true Ishmaelite; for in the desert, learning, good faith, and hospitality can still be found—at least, so Arabs say.

Orange and azofaifa trees, with almonds, sweet limes and walnuts, stood up against the waning light, outlined in the clear atmosphere almost so sharply as to wound the eye.

Around the well goats and sheep lay, whilst a girl led a camel round the Noria track; women sat here and there and gossiped with their tall earthenware jars stuck by the point into the ground, and waited for their turn, just as they did in the old times, so far removed from us, but which in Arab life is but as yesterday, when Jacob cheated Esau, and the whole scheme of Arab life was photographed for us by the writers of the Pentateuch. In fact, the self-same scene which has been acted every evening for two thousand years throughout North Africa, since the adventurous ancestors of the tribesmen of to-day left Hadrumut or Yemen, and upon which Allah looks down approvingly, as recognising that the traditions of his first recorded life have been well kept. Next day he trotted through the barren plain of Seddat, the Jibel Saghra making a black line on the horizon to the south. Here Berber tribes sweep in their razzias like hawks; but who would plunder a rekass carrying a bowl of fish? Crossing the dreary plain and dreaming of his entry into Tafilet, which now was almost in his reach not two days distant, the sun beating on his head, the water almost boiling in the bowl, hungry and footsore, and in the state betwixt waking and sleep into which those who smoke hemp on journeys often get, he branched away upon a trail leading towards the south. Between the oases of Todghra and Ferkla, nothing but stone and sand, black stones on yellow sand; sand, and yet more sand, and then again stretches of blackish rocks with a suddra bush or two, and here and there a colocynth, bitter and beautiful as love or life, smiling up at the traveller from amongst the stones. Towards midday the path led towards a sandy tract all overgrown with sandrac bushes and crossed by trails of jackals and hyenas, then it quite disappeared, and Amarabat waking from his dream saw he was lost. Like a good shepherd, his first thought was for his fish; for he imagined the last few hours of sun had made them faint, and one of them looked heavy and swam sideways, and the rest kept rising to the surface in an uneasy way. Not for a moment was Amarabat frightened, but looked about for some known landmark, and finding none started to go back on his trail. But to his horror the wind which always sweeps across the Sahara had covered up his tracks, and on the stony paths which he had passed his feet had left no prints. Then Amarabat, the first moments of despair passed by, took a long look at the horizon, tightened his belt, pulled up his slipper heels, covered his precious bowl with a corner of his robe, and started doggedly back upon the road he thought he traversed on the deceitful path. How long he trotted, what he endured, whether the fish died first, or if he drank, or, faithful to the last, thirsting met death, no one can say. Most likely wandering in the waste of sandhills and of suddra bushes he stumbled on, smoking his hashish while it lasted, turning to Mecca at the time of prayer, and trotting on more feebly (for he was born to run), till he sat down beneath the sundried bushes where the Shinghiti on his Mehari found him dead beside the trail. Under a stunted sandarac tree, the head turned to the east, his body lay, swollen and distorted by the pangs of thirst, the tongue protruding rough as a parrot's, and beside him lay the seven golden fish, once bright and shining as the pure gold when the goldsmith pours it molten from his pot, but now turned black and bloated, stiff, dry, and dead. Life the mysterious, the mocking, the inscrutable, unseizable, the uncomprehended essence of nothing and of everything, had fled, both from the faithful messenger and from his fish. But the Khalifa's parting caution had been well obeyed, for by the tree, unbroken, the crystal bowl still glistened beautiful as gold, in the fierce rays of the Saharan sun.

IT IS WRITTEN

ALL Tangier knew the Rubio, the fair-haired blind man, who sat upon the mounting-block outside the stables of the principal hotel. His bright red hair and bleared blue eyes, together with his freckled face, looking just like a newly scalded pig, had given him the name by which the Europeans knew him, although no doubt he was Mohammed, something or another, amongst his brethren in the faith.

He spoke indifferently well most European languages up to a point, and perfectly as far as blasphemy or as obscenity was concerned, and his quick ear enabled him as if by magic to ascertain the nationality of any European passer-by, if ever he had spoken to the man before, and to salute him in his mother-tongue.

All day he sat, amused and cheerful, in the sun. Half faun, half satyr, his blindness kept him from entire materialism, giving him sometimes a half-spiritual air, which possibly may have been but skin deep, and of the nature of the reflection of a sunset on a dunghill; or again, may possibly have been the true reflection of his soul as it peeped through the dunghill of the flesh.

As people passed along the road, their horses slithering and sliding on the sharp pitch of the paved road, which dips straight down from underneath the mounting-block of the hotel, between the tapia walls, over which bougainvilleas peep, down to the Soko Grande, El Rubio would hail them, as if he had been a dark lighthouse, set up to guide their steps.

Occasionally, but rarely, he mistook his mark, hailing some European lady with obscenity, or bawling to the English clergyman that he could tell him "where one fine girl live, not more than fifteen year"; but his contrition was so manifest, when he found his mistake, that no one bore him malice, and he remained an institution of the place and a perpetual rent-charge on all passers-by.

By one of the strange contradictions which Nature seems to take delight in just to confound us, when after a few thousand years of study we think we know her ways, the Rubio had a love of horses which in him replaced the usual love of music of the blind. No one could hold two or three fighting stallions better, and few Moors in all the place were bolder riders—that is, on roads he knew. Along the steep and twisting path that leads towards Spartel he used to ride full speed and shouting "Balak" when he was sent upon a message or with a horse from town out to the villas on the hill. All those who knew him left him a free road, and if he met a herd of cattle or of sheep, the horse would pick his way through them, twisting and turning of his own accord, whilst his blind rider left the reins upon his neck and galloped furiously. In what dark lane or evil-smelling hole he lived no European knew. Always well dressed and clean, he lived apart both from the Moors and from the Europeans, and in a way from all humanity, passing his time, as does a lizard, in the sun and in the evening disappearing to his den. The missions of the various true faiths, Catholic, Presbyterian, and Anglican, had tackled him in vain. Whether it was that none of them had anything to offer which he thought better than the cheerful optimism with which he was endowed by nature to fight the darkness of the world he lived in, is difficult to say. Still, they had all been worsted; not that the subject of their spiritual blandishments could have been termed a strict Mohammedan, for he drank any kind of spirits that was presented to him by Christians, anxious perhaps to make him break the spirit, if they were impotent to move him in the letter of his law. Still though he sat with nothing seemingly reflected on the retina of his opaque and porcelain-coloured eyes, his interior vision was as keen or keener than that of other men. He never seemed a man apart, or cut off from his fellows, but had his place in life, just as throughout the East the poorest and most miserable appear to have, not barred out from mankind by mere externals as are their brethren in the North, shut in the ice of charity, as bees are shut behind a plate of glass so that the rich may watch their movements in the hive.

Up from the Arab market over which he sat, as it were presiding in his darkness, just as God seems to sit, presiding blindly, over a world which either mocks Him, or is mocked at by Him, there came a breath of Eastern life, bearing a scent compounded of the acrid sweat of men, dried camel's dung, of mouldering charcoal fires, of spices, gunpowder, and of a thousand simples, all brought together by mere chance or fate, a sort of incense burned in his honour, and agreeable to his soul. It seemed to bring him life, and put him into touch with all he could not see, but yet could feel, almost as well as if he saw, just as did other men.

Sniffing it up, his nostrils would dilate, and then occasionally a shadow crossed his face, and as he ran his hands down the legs of the horse left in his charge, marking acutely any splint or spavin they might have, he used to mutter, half in a resigned, half in an irritated way, "Mektub," the sole profession of his faith that he was ever heard to make, for if a thing is written down by fate, it follows naturally that there is somebody who writes, if only foolishly. Whether the mystic phrase of resignation referred to his condition or to the possible splint upon the horse's leg, no one could tell, but as the shadow passed away, as quickly as it came, he soon fell back again into the half-resigned good humour of the blind, which, like the dancer's lithographic smile, seems quite involuntary.

Years melted into one another, and time sauntered by, just as it always must have sauntered in the town where hours are weeks, weeks months, and months whole years, and still the hum of animals and men rose from the Arab market, and still the shadows in the evening creeping on the sand seemed something tangible to the blind watcher on his stone. Not

that he cared for time, or even marked its flight, or would
have cared to mark it, had it been pointed out to him, for life
was pleasant, the springs of charity unfailing, wit ever present
in his brain, and someone always had a horse to hold, to
which he talked, as it stood blinking in the sun. His blindness did not seem to trouble him, and if he thought of it at
all, he looked on it as part and parcel of the scheme of nature,
against which it is impious to contend. Doctors had peered
into his eyes with lenses, quarrelled with one another on their
diagnoses of his case, and still the Rubio sat contented,
questioning nothing, and enduring everything, sun, rain,
wind, flies, and dust, as patiently as if he were a rock. Nothing
was further from his thoughts than that he ever once again
could see. Plainly, it had been written in the books of fate he
should be blind, and so when European doctors talked to
him of operations and the like, he smiled, not wishing to
offend. and never doubting of their learning for had not one
of them cured a relation of his own of intermittent fever by
the use of some white magic powder when native doctors,
after having burned him with a red-hot iron and made him
take texts of the Koran steeped in water had ignominiously
failed?

All that they said did not appeal to him for all of them
were serious men who talked the matter over gravely and
looked on him as something curious on which to exercise
their skill. All might have gone on in the same old way and
to this day the Rubio still sat upon his stone without a wish to
see the horses that he held the sunlight falling white upon the
towers or the red glare upon the Spanish coast at eventide,
had not a German scientist appeared on the horizon of his
life.

From the first day on which the Rubio held the doctor's
horse a fellowship sprang up between them, not easy to
explain. No single word of Arabic the doctor spoke, and all
the German that the Rubio knew was either objurgatory or
obscene, and yet the men were friends. Tall and uncouth and

with a beard that looked as if it never had been combed, his trousers short and frayed and with an inch or two of dirty sock showing between them and his shoes, dressed in a yellowish alpaca jacket, and a white solar topee lined with green, the doctor peered out on the world through neutral-tinted glasses, for his own eyes were weak.

Whether this weakness drew him to the blind, or if he liked to hear the Rubio's tales about the Europeans he had known, to all of whom he gave the worst of characters, calling them drunkards and hinting at dark vices which he averred they practised to a man—not that he for a moment believed a single word he uttered, but thought apparently his statements gave a piquancy to conversation—the doctor never said. Soon Tangier knew him for a character, and as he stumbled on his horse about the town, curing the Arabs of ophthalmia and gathering facts for the enormous book he said he meant to write upon North Africa, his reputation grew. The natives christened him "Father of Blindness," which name appeared to him a compliment, and he would use it, speaking of himself, complacently, just as a Scotsman likes to be spoken of under the style and title of the land he owns, although it be all bog. Though in the little world of men in which he lived the doctor was a fool, in the large field of science he was competent enough, and when he proved to demonstration to the other doctors in the place that a slight operation would restore the Rubio's sight, they all fell in with it, and though for years the object of their care had held their horses and they had seen him every day, without observing him, he now became of interest, just as a moth becomes of interest when it is dead and put into a case with other specimens.

Whether the sympathy that certainly exists between wise men and those whose intellect is rudimentary, and which is rarely manifested between a learned and an ordinary man, prevailed upon the Rubio to submit himself to the ministrations of the German man of science, Allah alone can tell. A season saw the mounting-block deserted, and tourists gave their horses to be held by boys, who tied them by the reins to rings high in the wall, and fell asleep, leaving the animals to fight and break their bridles, and for a time no stream of cheerful blasphemy was heard, in any European tongue, upon the mounting-stone. In a clean unaccustomed bed in a dark corner of Hope House, the missionary hospital, the Rubio lay, his head bound up in bandages, silent, but cheerful, confident in the skill of his strange friend, but yet incredulous, after the Arab way.

During the long six weeks, what were his thoughts and expectations it is difficult to say. Perhaps they ran upon the wonders of the new world he would inherit with his sight, perhaps he rather dreaded to behold all that he knew so well and so familiarly by touch. He who, when like a lizard he had basked against his wall, had never for a moment ceased from talking, now was silent, and when the doctor visited him, to dress his eyes, and make his daily diagnosis of the case, answered to all the words of hope he heard, "It will be, as God wishes it to be," and turned uneasily between his unfamiliar sheets. At last the day arrived when doctors judged the necessary time had passed. No one in Tangier was more confident than was the "Father of Blindness," who went and came about the town buoyed high with expectation, for he was really a kind-hearted man, learned but simple, after the fashion of his kind.

At early morning all was ready, and in the presence of the assembled doctors of the place with infinite precaution the dressings were removed. Cautiously and by degrees, a little light was let into the room. Holding his patient's hand and visibly moved, the German asked him if he saw. "Not yet," the Rubio answered, and then, throwing the window open wide, the sunlight filled the room, falling upon the figure in the bed, and on the group of doctors standing by expectantly. It filled the room, and through the window showed the mountains standing out blue above Tarifa, and the strait, calm as a sheet of glass, except where the two "Calas" cut it into foam. It fell upon the cliffs which jut into the sea below Hope House; upon the hills of Anjera, and on the bird-like sails of the feluccas in the bay, filling the world with gladness that a new day was born. Still on his bed the Rubio lay, pale with his long confinement, and with his hands nervously feeling at his eyes. All saw that the experiment had failed, and with a groan the German man of science buried his head between his hands and sobbed aloud, the tears dimming his spectacles and running down upon his beard. With a grave smile the patient got out of his bed, and having felt his way to where he heard the sobs, laid his rough, freckled hand upon the shoulder of his friend, and said as unconcernedly, as if he had not suffered in the least, "Weep not; it was not written"; then looking round, asked for a boy to lead him back again to his accustomed seat upon his stone.

FAITH

"I TOLD you," said Hamed-el-Angeri, "of how once on a time all beasts could speak, and of how Allah, in his might, and for his glory, and no doubt for some wise cause, rendered them dumb, or at least caused them to lose their Arabic. Now will I tell you of a legend of the Praised One who sleepeth in Medina, and whom alone Allah has pardoned of all men."

He paused, and the hot sun streamed through the branches of the carob tree, under whose shade we sat upon a rug, during the hottest hours, and threw his shadow on the sandy soil, drawing him, long of limb, and lithe of pose, like John the Baptist revealed by Donatello in red clay.

Our horses hung their heads, and from the plain a mist of heat arose, dancing and shivering in the air, as the flame dances waveringly from a broken gas-pipe lighted by workmen in a street. Grasshoppers twittered, raising their pandean pipe of praise to Allah for his heat, and now and then a locust whirred across the sky, falling again into the hard dry grass, just as a flying-fish falls out of sight into the sea. "They say," Hamed again began, "that in Medina, or in Mecca, in the blessed days when God spake to his Prophet, and he composed his book, making his laws, and laying down his rules of conduct for men's lives, that many wondered that no nook or corner in all Paradise was set apart for those who bore us, or whose milk we sucked, when they had passed their prime."

Besides the Perfect Four, women there were who with the light that Allah gave them, strove to be faithful, just, and loving, and to do their duty as it seemed to them, throughout their lives.

One there was, Rahma, a widow, who had borne four stalwart sons, all slain in battle, and who, since their deaths, had kept herself in honour and repute, labouring all day with distaff and with loom.

Seated in a lost dúar in the hills, she marvelled much that the wise son of Ámina, he to whom the word of God had been vouchsafed, and who himself had owed his fortune to a woman, could be unjust. Long did she ponder in her hut beyond Medina, and at last resolved to take her ass, and set forth, even to Mecca, and there speak with God's messenger, and hear from him the why and wherefore of the case. She set her house in order, leaving directions to the boy who watched her goats to tend them diligently, and then upon the lucky day of all the week, that Friday upon which the faithful all assemble to give praise, she took her way.

The people of the village thought her mad, as men in every age have always thought all those demented who have determined upon any course which has not entered into their own dull brains. Wrinkled and withered like a mummy, draped in her shroud-like haik, she sat upon her ass. A bag of dates, with one of barley, and a small water-skin her luggage, and in her heart that foolish, generous, undoubting Arab faith, powerful enough to move the most stupendous mountain chain of facts which weigh down European souls, she journeyed on.

Rising before the dawn, in the cold chill of desert nights, she fed the beast from her small store of corn, shivering and waiting for the sun to warm the world. Then, as the first faint flush of pink made palm trees look like ghosts and half revealed the mountain tops floating above a sea of mist, she turned towards the town, wherein he dwelt who denied Paradise to all but girls, and prayed. Then, drawing out her bag of dates, she ate, with the content of those to whom both appetite and food are not perennial gifts.

As the day broke, and the fierce sun rose, as it seemed with his full power, the enemy of those who travel in those wilds, she clambered stiffly to her seat on her straw pillion, and with a suddra thorn urged on her ass to a fast stumbling walk, his feet seeming but scarce to leave the ground as he bent forward his meek head as if he bore the sins of all mankind upon his back.

The dew lay thickly on the scant mimosa scrub and camel-thorn, bringing out aromatic odours, and filling the interstices of spiders' webs as snow fills up the skeletons of leaves. The colocynths growing between the stones seemed frosted with the moisture of the dawn, and for a brief half-hour nature was cool, and the sun shone in vain. Then, as by magic, all the dew disappeared, and the fierce sunlight heated the stones, and turned the sand to fire.

Green lizards, with kaleidoscopic tints, squattered across the track, and hairy spiders waddled in and out the stones. Scorpions and centipedes revived, and prowled about like sharks or tigers looking for their prey, whilst beetles, rolling balls of camels' dung, strove to as little purpose as do men, who, struggling in the dung of business, pass their lives, like beetles, with their eyes fixed upon the ground.

As the sun gradually gained strength, the pilgrim drew her tattered haik about her face, and sat, a bundle of white rags, head crouched on her breast and motionless, except the hand holding the reins, which half mechanically moved up and down, as she urged on the ass into a shuffling trot.

The hot hours caught her under a solitary palm tree, by a half-stagnant stream, in which great tortoises put up their heads, and then sank out of sight as noiselessly as they had risen, leaving a trail of bubbles on the slimy pool. Some red flamingos lazily took flight, and then with outstretched wings descended further off, and stood expectant, patient as fishers, and wrapt in contemplation during the mysteries of their gentle craft.

Then the full silence of the desert noontide fell upon the scene, as the old woman, after having tied her ass's feet with a thin goat's-hair cord, sat down to rest. Long did she listen to her ass munching his scanty feed of corn, and then the cricket's chirp and the faint rustling of the lone palm-trees' leaves lulled her to sleep.

Slumbering, she dreamed of her past life—for dreams are but the shadow of the past, reflected on the mirror of the brain—and saw herself, a girl, watching her goats, happy to lie beneath a bush all day, eating her bread dipped in the brook at noon, and playing on a reed; then, evening come, driving her charges home, to sleep on the hard ground upon a sheepskin, in the corner of the tent. She saw herself a maiden, not wondering overmuch at the new view of life which age had brought, accepting in the same way as did her goats, that she too must come under the law of nature, and in pain bear sons. Next, marriage, with its brief feasting, an eternal round of grinding corn, broken alone by childbirth once a year, during the period of her youth. Then came the one brief day of joy since she kept goats a child upon the hills, the morning when she bore a son, one who would be a man, and ride, and fill his father's place upon the earth.

She saw her sons grow up, her husband die, and then her children follow him, herself once more alone, and keeping goats upon the hill, only brown, bent and wrinkled, instead of round, upright and rosy, as when she was a child. Still, with the resignation of her race, a resignation as of rocks to rain, she did not murmur, but took it all just as her goats bore all things, yielding their necks, almost, as it were, cheerfully, to her blunt knife, upon the rare occasions when she found herself constrained to kill one for her food.

Waking and dozing, she passed through the hottest hours when even palm trees drooped, and the tired earth appears to groan under the fury of the sun.

Then rising up refreshed, she led her ass to water at the stream, watching him drink amongst the stones, whitened with the salt scum, which in dry seasons floats upon all rivers in that land.

Mounting she struck into the sandy deep-worn track

which, fringed with feathery tamarisks, led out into the plain. Like a faint cloud on the horizon rose the white city where the Prophet dwelt, and as the ass shuffled along, travellers from many paths passed by, and the road grew plainer as she advanced upon her way.

Horsemen, seated high above their horses in their chair saddles, ambled along, their spears held sloping backwards or trailing in the dust. Meeting each other on the way, they whirled and charged, drawing up short when near and going through the evolutions of the "Jerid," and then with a brief "Peace," again becoming grave and silent, they ambled on, their straight sharp spurs pressed to their horses' sides.

Camels with bales of goods, covered with sheepskin or with striped cloth, swayed onward in long lines, their heads moving alternately about, as if they were engaged in some strange dance. Asses, with piles of brushwood covering them to their ears, slid past like animated haystacks, and men on foot veiled to the eyes, barefooted, with their slippers in their hands, or wearing sandals, tramped along the road. Pack-mules, with bundles of chopped straw packed hard in nets, or carrying loads of fresh-cut barley or of grass, passed by, their riders sitting sideways on the loads, or, running at their tails with one hand on their quarters, seemed to push on their beasts, as with the curses, without which no mule will move, they whiled away the time. A fine red dust enveloped everything as in a sand storm, turning burnouses and haiks brown, and caking thickly on the sweaty faces of the men.

Nearing the city gates the crush grew thicker, till at last a constant stream of people blocked the way, jostling and pushing, but good-humouredly, after the way of those to whom time is the chiefest property they own.

Dark rose the crenellated walls, and the white gate made a strange blot of light in the surrounding brown of plain and roads and mud-built houses of the town.

Entering upon the cobbled causeway, she passed through the gate, and in a corner, squatting on the ground, saw the scribes writing, the spearmen lounging in the twisted passage with their spears stacked against the wall. Then the great rush of travellers bore her as on a wave into the precincts of the town.

She rode by heaps of rubbish, on which lay chickens and dead dogs, with scraps of leather, camel's bones, and all the jetsam of a hundred years, burned by the sun till they became innocuous, but yet sending out odours which are indeed the very perfumes of Araby the blest.

Huts made of canes, near which grew castor-oil plants, fringed the edge of the high dunghill of the town, and round it curs, lean, mangy, and as wild as jackals, slept with a bloodshot eye half open, ready to rush and bark at anyone who ventured to infringe upon the limits of their sphere of influence.

She passed the sandy horse-market, where auctioneers, standing up in their stirrups with a switch between their teeth, circled and wheeled their horses as a seagull turns upon the wing, or, starting them full speed, stopped them with open mouth and foam-flecked bit, turned suddenly to statues, just at the feet of the impassive bystanders, who showed their admiration but by a guttural "Wah," or gravely interjected "Allah," as they endeavoured to press home some lie, too gross to pass upon its merits, even in that bright atmosphere of truth which in all lands encompasses the horse.

A second gate she passed, in which more tribesmen lounged, their horses hobbled, and themselves stretched out on mats, and the tired pilgrim found herself in a long cobbled street, on which her ass skated and slipped about, being accustomed to the desert sands. In it the dyers plied their craft, their arms stained blue or red, as they plunged hanks of wool into their vats, from which a thick dark steam rose, filling the air with vapours as from a solfatara, or such as rises from those islands in the west, known to those daring men "who ride that huge unwieldy beast, the sea, like fools, trembling upon its waves in hollow logs," and braving death upon that element which Allah has not given to his faithful to subdue. Smiths and artificers in brass and those who ply the bellows, sweating and keeping up a coil, unfit for council, but by whose labour and the wasting of whose frames cities are rendered stable, and states who cherish them set their foundations like wise builders on a rock, she passed.

Stopping, the pilgrim asked from a white-bearded man where in the city did the Prophet sit, and if the faithful, even the faithful such as she, had easy access to the person of the man whom God had chosen as his vicegerent upon earth.

Stroking his beard, the elder made reply: "Praise be to God, the One, our Lord Mohammed keeps no state. He sits within the mosque which we of Mecca call Masjida n'Nabi, with his companions, talking and teaching, and at times is silent, as his friends think, communing with the Lord. All can approach him, and if thou hast anything to ask, tether thine ass at the mosque door and go in boldly, and thou wilt be received."

The pilgrim gave "the Peace," and passed along in the dense crowd, in which camels and mules, with horses, negroes tribesmen, sellers of sweetmeats, beggars, and water-carriers, all swelled the press.

Again she entered into streets, streets, and more streets. She threaded through bazaars where saddle-makers wrought, bending the camel's shoulder-bones to form the trees, and stretching unshrunk mare's hide over all. Crouched in their booths they sat like josses in a Chinese temple, sewing elaborate patterns, plaiting stirrup leathers, and cutting out long Arab reins which dangle almost to the ground. Before their booths stood wild-eyed Bedouins, their hair worn long and greased with mutton fat till it shone glossy as a raven's wing. They chaffered long for everything they bought. Spurs, reins, or saddle-cloths were all important to them, therefore they took each piece up separately, appraised it to its disadvantage, and often made pretence to go away, calling down maledictions on the head of him who for his goods wished to be paid in life's blood of the poor. Yet they returned, and, after much expenditure of eloquence, bore off their purchase, as if they feared that robbers would deprive them of their prize, hiding it cautiously under the folds of their brown goat's-hair cloaks, or stowed in the recesses of their saddle-bags.

A smell of spices showed the tired wanderer that she approached the Kaiseria, wherein dwell those who deal in saffron, pepper, anise, and cummin, assafœtida, cloves, nutmegs, cinnamon, sugar and all the merchandise which is brought over sea by ship to Yembo, and then conveyed to Mecca and Medina upon camels' backs.

Stopping an instant where a Jaui had his wares displayed, she bought an ounce of semsin, knowing Abdallah's son had three things specially in which he took delight, women, scents, and meat, but not knowing that of the first two, as his wife Ayesha said in years to come, he had his fill, but never of the third. The Kaiseria left behind, she felt her heart beat as she neared the mosque.

Simple it stood on a bare space of sand, all made of palm-trees hewn foursquare, the walls of cane and of mud, the roof of palm leaves over the mihrab—simple and only seven cubits high, and yet a fane in which the pæan to the God of Battles echoed so loudly that its last blast was heard in Aquitaine, in farthest Hind, Irac, in China, and by the marshy shores of the Lake Chad.

As she drew near the mosque not knowing (as a woman) how to pray, she yet continued muttering something which, whilst no doubt strengthening her soul, was to the full as acceptable to the One God as it were framed after the strictest canon of the Moslem law. Then, sliding to the ground, she tied her ass's feet with a palmetto cord, and taking in her hand her ounce of semsin as an offering passed into the court.

Under the orange trees a marble fountain played, stained

here and there with time, murmuring its never-ending prayer, gladdening the souls of men with its faint music, and serving as a drinking-place to countless birds, who, after drinking, washed, and then, flying back to the trees, chanted their praises to the giver of their lives.

A little while she lingered, and then, after the fashion of her race, which, desert born, cannot pass running water, even if they are being led to death, without a draught, she stopped and drank. Then, lifting up her eyes, she saw a group seated beneath a palm tree, and at once felt her eyes had been considered worthy to behold the man whom, of all men, his Maker in his life had pardoned and set His seal upon his shoulder as a memorial of His grace.

As she drew near she marked the Prophet, the Promised, the Blessed One, who in the middle of his friends sat silently as they discussed or prayed.

Of middle height he was and strongly made, his colour fair, his hair worn long and parted, neither exactly curling nor yet smooth, his beard well shaped and flecked with silver here and there, clipped close upon his upper lip; and about the whole man an air of neatness and of cleanliness. His dress was simple, for, hanging to the middle of his calf, appeared his undershirt, and over it he wore as it fell out upon that day, a fine striped mantle from the Yémen, which he wrapped round about him tightly after the fashion of a coat; his shoes, which lay beside him, were of the fashion of the Hadhramút, with thongs and clouted; his staff lay near to them, and as he spoke, he beat with his left hand upon the right, and often smiled so that his teeth appeared as white as hailstones, new fallen on the grass after an April storm.

Advancing to the group, the pilgrim gave "the Peace," and then tendering her offering, stood silent in the sight of all the company. Fear sealed her lips, and sweat ran down her cheeks as she gazed on the face of him to whom the Lord of Hosts had spoken, giving him power both to unloose and bind.

Gently he spoke, and lifting up his hand, said: "Mother, what is it you seek, and why this offering?"

Then courage came to her, and words which all the Arabs have at their command, and she poured forth her troubles, telling the prophet of her loneliness, her goats, her hut, of her lost husband and her sons all slain in battle, in the service of the Lord. She asked him why her sex was barred from Paradise, and if the prophet would exclude Ámina, she who bore him, from the regions of the blessed. With the direct and homely logic of her race, she pressed her claims.

Well did she set out woman's life, how she bore children in sore suffering, reared them in trouble and anxiety, moulded and formed their minds in childhood, as she had moulded and had formed their bodies in the womb.

When she had finished she stood silent, anxiously waiting a reply, whilst on the faces of the fellowship there came a look as if they too remembered those who in tents and dúars on the plains had nurtured them, but no one spoke, for the respect they bore to him who, simply clad as they, was yet superior to all created men.

Long did he muse, no doubt remembering Kadíja, and how she clave to him in evil and in good report, when all men scoffed, and then opening his lips he gave his judgment on the pilgrim's statement of the case.

"Allah," he said, "has willed it that no old woman enter Paradise, therefore depart, and go in peace, and trouble not the prophet of the Lord."

Tears rose to Rahma's eyes, and she stood turned to stone, and through the company there ran a murmur of compassion for her suffering. Then stretching out his hand, Mohammed smiled and said: "Mother, Allah has willed it as I declared to you, but as his power is infinite, at the last day, it may be he will make you young again, and you shall enter into the regions of the blessed, and sit beside the Perfect Ones, the four, who of all women have found favour in his sight."

He ceased, and opening the offered packet, took the

semsin in his hand, and eagerly inhaled the scent, and Rahma, having thanked him, stooped down and kissed the fringes of his striped Yemen mantle, then straightening herself as she had been a girl, passed through the courtyard, mounted on her ass and struck into the plain.

EL TANGO ARGENTINO

MOTOR-CARS swept up to the covered passage of the front door of the hotel, one of those international caravansaries that pass their clients through a sort of vulgarising process that blots out every type. It makes the Argentine, the French, the Englishman, and the American all alike before the power of wealth.

The cars surged up as silently as snow falls from a fir-tree in a thaw, and with the same soft swishing noise. Tall, liveried porters opened the doors (although, of course, each car was duly furnished with a footman) so nobly that any one of them would have graced any situation in the State.

The ladies stepped down delicately, showing a fleeting vision of a leg in a transparent stocking, just for an instant, through the slashing of their skirts. They knew that every man, their footman, driver, the giant watchers at the gate, and all who at the time were going into the hotel, saw and were moved by what they saw just for a moment; but the fact did not trouble them at all. It rather pleased them, for the most virtuous feel a pleasurable emotion when they know that they excite. So it will be for ever, for thus and not by votes alone they show that they are to the full men's equals, let the law do its worst.

Inside the hotel, heated by steam, and with an atmosphere of scent and flesh that went straight to the head just as the fumes of whisky set a drinker's nerves agog, were seated all the finest flowers of the cosmopolitan society of the French capital.

Lesbos had sent its legions, and women looked at one another appreciatively, scanning each item of their neighbour's clothes, and with their colour heightening when by chance their eyes met those of another priestess of their sect.

Rich rastaquaoures, their hats too shiny, and their boots too tight, their coats fitting too closely, their sticks mounted with great gold knobs, walked about or sat at little tables, all talking strange varieties of French.

Americans, the men apparently all run out of the same mould, the women apt as monkeys to imitate all that they saw in dress, in fashion and in style, and more adaptable than any other women in the world from lack of all traditions, conversed in their high nasal tones. Spanish-Americans from every one of the Republics were well represented, all talking about money: of how Doña Fulana Perez had given fifteen hundred francs for her new hat, or Don Fulano had just scored a million on the Bourse.

Jews and more Jews, and Jewesses and still more Jewesses, were there, some of them married to Christians and turned Catholic, but betrayed by their Semitic type, although they talked of Lourdes and of the Holy Father with the best.

After the "five-o'clock," turned to a heavy meal of toast and buns, of Hugel loaf, of sandwiches, and of hot cake, the scented throng, restored by the refection after the day's hard work of shopping, of driving here and there like souls in purgatory to call on people that they detested, and other labours of a like nature, slowly adjourned to a great hall in which a band was playing. As they walked through the passages, men pressed close up to women and murmured in their ears, telling them anecdotes that made them flush and giggle as they protested in an unprotesting style. Those were the days of the first advent of the Tango Argentino, the dance that since has circled the whole world, as it were, in a movement of the hips. Ladies pronounced it charming as they half closed their eyes and let a little shiver run across their lips. Men said it was the only dance that was worth dancing. It was so Spanish, so unconventional, and combined all the æsthetic movements of the figures on an Etruscan vase with the strange grace of the Hungarian gipsies . . . it was so, as one may say, so . . . as you may say . . . you know.

When all were seated, the band, Hungarians, of course—oh, those dear gipsies!—struck out into a rhythm, half ragtime, half habanera, canaille, but sensuous, and hands involuntarily, even the most aristocratic hands—of ladies whose immediate progenitors had been pork-packers in Chicago, or gambusinos who had struck it rich in Zacatecas—tapped delicately, but usually a little out of time, upon the backs of chairs.

A tall young man, looking as if he had got a holiday from a tailor's fashion plate, his hair sleek, black and stuck down to his head with a cosmetic, his trousers so immaculately creased they seemed cut out of cardboard, led out a girl dressed in a skirt so tight that she could not have moved in it had it not been cut open to the knee.

Standing so close that one well-creased trouser leg disappeared in the tight skirt, he clasped her round the waist, holding her hand almost before her face. They twirled about, now bending low, now throwing out a leg, and then again revolving, all with a movement of the hips that seemed to blend the well-creased trouser and the half-open skirt into one inharmonious whole. The music grew more furious and the steps multiplied, till with a bound the girl threw herself for an instant into the male dancer's arms, who put her back again upon the ground with as much care as if she had been a new-laid egg, and the pair bowed and disappeared.

Discreet applause broke forth, and exclamations such as "wonderful," "what grace," "Vivent les espagnols," for the discriminating audience took no heed of independence days, of mere political changes and the like, and seemed to think that Buenos Aires was a part of Spain, never having heard of San Martin, Bolivar, Paez, and their fellow-liberators.

Paris, London and New York were to that fashionable crowd the world, and anything outside—except, of course, the Hungarian gipsies and the Tango dancers—barbarous and beyond the pale.

After the Tango came "La Maxixe brésilienne," rather more languorous and more befitting to the dwellers in the tropics than was its cousin from the plains. Again the discreet applause broke out, the audience murmuring "charming," that universal adjective that gives an air of being in a perpetual pastrycook's when ladies signify delight. Smiles and sly glances at their friends showed that the dancers' efforts at indecency had been appreciated.

Slowly the hall and tea-rooms of the great hotel emptied themselves, and in the corridors and passages the smell of scent still lingered, just as stale incense lingers in a church.

Motor-cars took away the ladies and their friends, and drivers, who had shivered in the cold whilst the crowd inside sweated in the central heating, exchanged the time of day with the liveried doorkeepers, one of them asking anxiously: "Dis, Anatole, as-tu vu mes vaches?"

With the soft closing of a well-hung door the last car took its perfumed freight away, leaving upon the steps a group of men, who remained talking over or, as they would say, undressing all the ladies who had gone.

"Argentine Tango, eh?" I thought, after my friends had left me all alone. Well, well, it has changed devilishly upon its passage overseas, even discounting the difference of the setting of the place where first I saw it danced so many years ago. So, sauntering down, I took a chair far back upon the terrace of the Café de la Paix, so that the sellers of *La Patrie*, and the men who have some strange new toy, or views of Paris in a long album like a broken concertina, should not tread upon my toes.

Over a Porto Blanc and a Brazilian cigarette, lulled by the noise of Paris and the raucous cries of the street-vendors, I fell into a doze.

Gradually the smell of petrol and of horse-dung, the two most potent fumes in our modern life, seemed to be blown away. Dyed heads and faces scraped till they looked blue as a baboon's; young men who looked like girls, with painted faces and with mincing airs; the raddled women, ragged men, and hags huddled in knitted shawls, lame horses, and taxi-cab drivers sitting nodding on their boxes —all faded into space, and from the nothing that is the past arose another scene.

I saw myself with Witham and his brother, whose name I have forgotten, Eduardo Peña, Congreve, and Eustaquio Medina, on a small rancho in an elbow of the great River Yi. The rancho stood upon a little hill. A quarter of a mile or so away the dense and thorny monte of hard-wood trees that fringed the river seemed to roll up towards it like a sea. The house was built of yellow pine sent from the United States. The roof was shingled, and the rancho stood planked down upon the plain, looking exactly like a box. Some fifty yards away stood a thatched hut that served as kitchen, and on its floor the cattle herders used to sleep upon their horse-gear with their feet towards the fire.

The corrals for horses and for sheep were just a little farther off, and underneath a shed a horse stood saddled day in, day out, and perhaps does so yet, if the old rancho still resists the winds.

Four or five horses, saddled and bridled, stood tied to a great post, for we were just about to mount to ride a league or two to a Baile, at the house of Frutos Barragán. Just after sunset we set out, as the sweet scent that the grasses of the plains send forth after a long day of heat perfumed the evening air.

The night was clear and starry, and above our heads was hung the Southern Cross. So bright the stars shone out that one could see almost a mile away; but yet all the perspective of the plains and woods was altered. Hillocks were sometimes indistinguishable, at other times loomed up like houses. Woods seemed to sway and heave, and by the sides of streams bunches of Pampa grass stood stark as sentinels, their feathery tufts looking like plumes upon an Indian's lance.

The horses shook their bridles with a clear, ringing sound as they stepped double, and their riders, swaying lightly in their seats, seemed to form part and parcel of the animals they rode.

Now and then little owls flew noiselessly beside us, circling above our heads, and then dropped noiselessly upon a bush. Eustaquio Medina, who knew the district as a sailor knows the seas where he was born, rode in the front of us. As his horse shied at a shadow on the grass or at the bones of some dead animal, he swung his whip round ceaselessly, until the moonlight playing on the silver-mounted stock seemed to transform it to an aureole that flickered about his head. Now and then somebody dismounted to tighten up his girth, his horse twisting and turning round uneasily the while, and, when he raised his foot towards the stirrup, starting off with a bound.

Time seemed to disappear and space be swallowed in the intoxicating gallop, so that when Eustaquio Medina paused for an instant to strike the crossing of a stream, we felt annoyed with him, although no hound that follows a hot scent could have gone truer on his line.

Dogs barking close at hand warned us our ride was almost over, and as we galloped up a rise Eustaquio Medina pulled up and turned to us.

"There is the house," he said, "just at the bottom of the hollow, only five squares away," and as we saw the flicker of the lights, he struck his palm upon his mouth after the Indian fashion, and raised a piercing cry. Easing his hand, he drove his spurs into his horse, who started with a bound into full speed, and as he galloped down the hill we followed him, all yelling furiously.

Just at the hitching-post we drew up with a jerk, our horses snorting as they edged off sideways from the black shadow that it cast upon the ground. Horses stood about everywhere, some tied and others hobbled, and from the house there came the strains of an accordion and the tinkling of guitars.

Asking permission to dismount, we hailed the owner of the house, a tall, old Gaucho, Frutos Barragán, as he stood waiting by the door, holding a *mate* in his hand. He bade us welcome, telling us to tie our horses up, not too far out of sight, for, as he said, "It is not good to give facilities to rogues, if they should chance to be about."

In the low, straw-thatched rancho, with its eaves blackened by the smoke, three or four iron bowls, filled with mare's fat, and with a cotton wick that needed constant trimming, stuck upon iron cattle-brands, were burning fitfully.

They cast deep shadows in the corners of the room, and when they flickered up occasionally the light fell on the dark and sun-tanned faces of the tall, wiry Gauchos and the light cotton dresses of the women as they sat with their chairs tilted up against the wall. Some thick-set Basques, an Englishman or two in riding breeches, and one or two Italians made up the company. The floor was earth, stamped hard till it shone like cement, and as the Gauchos walked upon it, their heavy spurs clinked with a noise like fetters as they trailed them on the ground.

An old, blind Paraguayan played on the guitar, and a huge negro accompanied him on an accordion. Their united efforts produced a music which certainly was vigorous enough, and now and then, one or the other of them broke into a song, high-pitched and melancholy, which, if you listened to it long enough, forced you to try to imitate its wailing melody and its strange intervals.

Fumes of tobacco and rum hung in the air, and of a strong and heady wine from Catalonia, much favoured by the ladies, which they drank from a tumbler, passing it to one another, after the fashion of a grace-cup at a City dinner, with great gravity. At last the singing ceased, and the orchestra struck up a Tango, slow, marked, and rhythmical.

Men rose, and, taking off their spurs, walked gravely to the corner of the room where sat the women huddled together as if they sought protection from each other, and with a compliment led them out upon the floor. The flowing poncho and the loose chiripá, which served as trousers, swung about just as the tartans of a Highlander swing as he dances, giving an air of ease to all the movements of the Gauchos as they revolved, their partners' heads peeping above their shoulders, and their hips moving to and fro.

At times they parted, and set to one another gravely, and then the man, advancing, clasped his partner round the waist and seemed to push her backwards, with her eyes half-closed and an expression of beatitude. Gravity was the keynote of the scene, and though the movements of the dance were as significant as it was possible for the dancers to achieve, the effect was graceful, and the soft, gliding motion and the waving of the parti-coloured clothes, wild and original, in the dim, flickering light.

Rum flowed during the intervals. The dancers wiped the perspiration from their brows, the men with the silk handkerchiefs they wore about their necks, the women with their sleeves. Tangos, *cielitos*, and *pericones* succeeded one another, and still the atmosphere grew thicker, and the lights seemed to flicker through a haze, as the dust rose from the mud floor. Still the old Paraguayan and the negro kept on playing with the sweat running down their faces, smoking and drinking rum in their brief intervals of rest, and when the music ceased for a moment, the wild neighing of a horse tied in the moonlight to a post, sounded as if he called his master to come out and gallop home again.

The night wore on, and still the negro and the Paraguayan stuck at their instruments. Skirts swung and ponchos waved, whilst *mate* circulated amongst the older men as they stood grouped about the door.

Then came a lull, and as men whispered in their partners' ears, telling them, after the fashion of the Gauchos, that they were lovely, their hair like jet, their eyes bright as "las tres Marias," and all the compliments which in their case were stereotyped and handed down for generations, loud voices rose, and in an instant two Gauchos bounded out upon the floor.

Long silver-handled knives were in their hands, their ponchos wrapped round their left arms served them as bucklers, and as they crouched, like cats about to spring, they poured out blasphemies.

"Stop this!" cried Frutos Barragán; but even as he spoke a knife-thrust planted in the stomach stretched one upon the floor. Blood gushed out from his mouth, his belly fell like a pricked bladder, and a dark stream of blood trickled upon the ground as he lay writhing in his death agony.

The iron bowls were overturned, and in the dark girls screamed and the men crowded to the door. When they emerged into the moonlight, leaving the dying man upon the floor, the murderer was gone; and as they looked at one another there came a voice shouting out: "Adios, Barragán! Thus does Vicente Castro pay his debts when a man tries to steal his girl," and the faint footfalls of an unshod horse galloping far out upon the plain.

I started, and the waiter standing by my side said: "Eighty centimes"; and down the boulevard echoed the harsh cry: "*La Patrie*, achetez *La Patrie*," and the rolling of the cabs.

UN MONSIEUR

IT may be the desire for sympathy that makes us yearn to pour our troubles into another's ear—how wise was the first Pope who hit upon auricular confession and made it sacred—that impelled Elise to tell the tale.

"He was," she said, "un monsieur, about fifty years of age, rich, dull, and only wanting wings to fly, so much he was puffed up with his position in the world and with his wealth.

"No, he did not treat me badly for some time, that is to say, after the visits that he used to pay me, he generally put a ten-pound note upon the mantelpiece and got into his motor with an air as of a Jupiter who had just parted from a Danae. After he went I usually took a bath, and then sat down to read Hérédia or Verlaine, some author or another of a kind that took me off into a world shut to such men as was my wealthy friend.

"He did not talk much; you see he was an Englishman, and seemed as if he was ashamed of speaking much to me, although of course that did not stop his visits to my house. I fancy that he regulated them on hygienic grounds, and rather thought he was a virtuous man in not allowing a full rein to what I feel assured he called the baser appetites . . . baser, eh? . . . the only ones he knew. He looked upon me, I am well aware, but as an instrument of pleasure, a sort of musical-box which he could set in motion with a ten-pound note.

"Upon my side I thought of him but as un monsieur, a man, that is, who, neither good nor bad, yet pushed by sensuality came to me at his stated intervals and went away appeased. His kisses bothered me, and all his efforts of what he perhaps called love were of a maladroit, that used to make me laugh . . . but then, in my profession, one gets to know what to expect of men.

"Of course he was quite unintellectual. The arts of every nature . . . love is an art"—and here she smiled and fluffed her hair out at the sides with conscious pride—"were but so many pastimes served up to him by men who lived by them. They all appeared to him a sort of intellectual 'saltimbanques,' I verily believe, and he must surely have referred to them as painters, poets, fiddlers, and all that kind of thing."

She paused, and the light falling on her fair wavy hair and on her well-kept hands gave her an air of such refinement that it was hard to think of her as the wage-slave of such a man as she had just described. Tall, slight, and well proportioned, blessed with the taste that seems the birthright of the women of her race, the little jewellery she wore appeared as much a portion of herself as the faint, half-professional smile that played about her lips, from the teeth outward, when she was talking to a man.

"You must not think," she said, "that I have laid the colour on too thickly; that would be inartistic. No, he was simply, as I said, un monsieur . . . not to use a vulgar word, which perhaps would have been better in his case.

"Ridiculous, of course—*cocasse;* I am not sure if there is any word in English that quite is the equivalent of that.

"Ludicrous, preposterous, no. . . . I mean he was absurd and had what we call 'une vraie tête de mari' . . . need I say more than that?

"All fat, rich men of fifty, when they make visits to such girls as me must of necessity be . . . *ah yes*, odd. To me the fact of being rich has something in it of itself that seems preposterous. Fancy how I must feel, who look on love as one of the fine arts, to have to *singer* it with a dull, fat, old man, simply because he has a big account at some bank or another! Apart from morals, to which I make no claim, it is an insult to the God who, I suppose, created both of us."

As she said this she drew herself up to her full height, hollowed her back a little like a gymnast on the horizontal bar, and then went on again.

"I had not seen my monsieur for a week or two and wondered what had happened to him, when a brougham with a pair of chestnut horses drew up at the door. Out of it got a lady, tall, dark, and with a sable cloak that must have cost an eye out of her head, elegant, svelte, well dressed and . . . beautiful. She did not give her name, but sent a message saying that she would like to see me, and when my maid had showed her up into the room she came forward and addressed me by my name . . . but charmingly, not stiffly in the least, and without any air of patronage. I asked her to be seated, and she sat down as naturally as if she had been on a visit to a woman of her own world, and after looking at me for a moment curiously, said in good French: 'I have come about a business matter.' I did not ask her how she knew my name, but merely smiled at her, with a slight inclination of the head, wondering internally what kind of business could have brought her, and as she paused a little as if she were debating what to say, I ran my eye over her, trying to recollect if I had seen her anywhere, but all to no avail. As we say, I undressed her, mentally, divining, as it were, she wore good stays and linen underneath. Her feet, of course, I saw, and her well-made French shoes and open-work silk stockings, and from her person generally there floated a faint odour of discreet perfume such as a woman of her world, who does not have to make men turn and look at her, can afford to wear.

"She certainly was beautiful and of my type, that is, the type that I admire, with dark and glossy hair in which you might have seen your face as in a looking-glass. All she had on I inwardly commended, her clothes and jewellery, though there was nothing in especial in the latter except a string of pearls, not large, like those in which a banker's wife or rich American, so to speak, hangs in chains, but finely shaped and dazzlingly white. All this review, of course, took but a minute, and as she did not speak a strange suspicion crossed my mind why she had come to see me, but as if she herself had read what thought was passing in my mind she blushed a little, making her look divine, and saying, 'It was on business that I came,' took from her muff a photograph, and holding it towards me asked me if I had ever seen the man.

"To my amazement, on looking at it I saw 'the man I have been telling you about, in all his commonness. His ears, just like an elephant's, his mottled face, and above all that air of thinking he was somebody only because he happened to be rich, all shouted at me.

"Still, every métier has its etiquette, and mine, just like a lawyer's or a priest's, is, or should be, discreet. I did not like the man, and on the other hand the lady was quite charming; but I stood firm, and, after looking at the thing indifferently, answered: 'I never saw the man,' and sat expectantly. A shadow of annoyance crossed the lady's face, and once again she came back to the charge.

" 'Are you quite sure?' she said, 'for I am told he is a friend of yours, and let me tell you I am rich.'

"This got my back up just a little, for it appeared as if I never should get clear of riches, and it amazed me, as it annoys me now, to see rich people go about trampling on honour and on everything by the mere weight of gold. Still, she was far too nice to quarrel with, so I sat quietly and smiled, and happening to catch her eye, we both stopped a half-laugh, and I, divining that she was my monsieur's wife, wondered what her next move would be to try and make me tell. After a word or two she got up from her chair, and going to the door paused for a minute as she held it in her hand, than turning to me smiling, said:

" 'I respect your honesty; but, after all, what does it matter whose money that it is you take? I will pay you anything up to a thousand pounds if you but choose to recollect.'

"Once more I thanked her, knowing, of course, that I was acting like a fool, but pleased to show her that I held honour above money—in spite of what I was. As she was going out she turned, and said again: 'Name your conditions'; and when I smiled and shook my head, she looked at me just for a moment, half with regret, half with approval, so that when finally she closed the door I felt, although she had not got her way, that she respected me for having made a stand against my interest.

"Three or four days had passed and the impression of the lady's visit had almost worn away, when who should come to see me but my friend.

"He looked so prosperous, and had so great an air as if the world might have belonged to him had he not been too lazy to write out a cheque . . . an oversight which, no doubt, when he had time enough, he still would rectify . . . I hardly found it in my heart at first to tell him what had passed. As soon, however, as he began what he perhaps called love-making and tried to draw me on to his knee, I, of course, seeing that he looked on the whole thing but as a hygienic visit, determined not to lose the chance.

"Therefore instead of letting, as I generally did, my head fall on his shoulder, closing my eyes, and thinking I was in the Calais steamer on a rough day, I pushed him off, and standing up, looked at him steadily between the eyes.

"He, for his part, knowing that he was going to pay for my complaisance, and having not an inkling of what was passing in my head, looked at me, half amazed, half puzzled, and exclaimed: 'Elise, old girl, what's up that you behave in this way to a pal?'

"Whether it was his confidence, a confidence that neither God nor Nature had given him the right to exercise with any woman upon earth, or whether I was revolted at my 'sale métier . . . car c'est un vrai métier de chien, tu sais,' I do not understand. When I had my hand free, for he tried to pull me to him and treat my attitude as a good joke, I said without a prelude: 'Your wife was here the other day.'

"He did not think I was in earnest and answered me in French, which he spoke fluently: 'Elle est bonne, celle-là.'

"However, when I had told him how his wife was dressed and named a bracelet that she wore he got more serious. I rather liked to tease him, and for a moment thought of saying something that would throw doubt upon his wife, but being also curious to find out what had been the real reason of her call, I merely said: 'She took your photograph out of her muff and showed it to me.'

"You never saw a man change quicker than my friend.

" 'What did you say, Elise?' he muttered; and when I told him that I had quite disclaimed all knowledge of him, he took my hand in his and kissed it, exclaiming: 'Elise, you are a splendid girl. . . . My wife wants to divorce me, but we have a child, a girl of ten, old enough to appreciate the disgrace of the Divorce Court, and I would give the world to spare her.'

"For the first time I rather liked him, for he spoke feelingly, and really seemed a man and not a money-bag. He drew me to him, and for the first time in my life I let him do so without repulsion, and holding both my hands he swore I had saved him, that he would do anything in the world for me, and if I wished to lead a different life and go back home to France that he would settle money on me to help me either to learn painting, which had always been my dream, or to get married to a decent man. When I had thanked him and he had kissed me several times, but quite as a man kisses a real woman and not as he had done before upon his visits, he went away, assuring me of his eternal gratitude, and turning at the door, just as his wife had done a day or two ago, to thank me once again. This time I was *bouleversée* and sat down and cried, thinking what I would do, and came to the conclusion to go to Paris and begin work in some atelier under some painter of repute. I thought of all that I should do—and for the life of art cannot, of course, be quite devoid of love—determined to choose some young painter or another, whom I should live with . . . quite en bourgeois, and darn his socks, and be as good to, for I am très bonne fille, as I have told you, as was possible.

"That was a happy afternoon, and my task, when in the

evening business sent me out to the Alhambra or some other music-hall, comparatively light. Days passed and weeks, then months, and still my grateful friend was silent, until one day, walking beside the Serpentine, I met him with his wife. He paled, and she looked at me quickly, and clutching at his arm, said: 'Tiens! C'est elle.'

"I made no sign, but fixed my eyes upon a child sailing his boat and passed on my way. That's all," said Elise; "and for the man, at first, I thought he was a lâche and then a scoundrel; but now I know he was but a rich man—'un monsieur'—and probably to-day, if he thinks of the matter now and then, promptly dismisses it, and says as he lights up a big cigar: 'She was a prostitute.' ''

UN AUTRE MONSIEUR

I HAD lost sight of Elise, said my friend, until one day as I was walking past, I am not sure if it was Woolland's or some other shop, I met her face to face. She seemed a little thin, I thought, and though she walked as gracefully as ever, holding her skirt up in the way that only her compatriots ever can compass, she looked so pale I saw that she was ill.

"What is the matter, Elise?" I said; "is it an affection of the heart?" To which she answered with a side look at the window of the shop to see if her hat was straight, "No, not of the heart; you forget that we professionals (she pronounced the word 'professionnelles') are quite impervious in that region; it is the chest I suffer from. The doctors say it is the life I have to lead—but really I have had congestion of the lungs."

We went to lunch just opposite in the grill-room of the hotel, where she insisted upon taking what she called "*La table de l'adultère*," for she declared as it was in a dark corner she had noticed several affairs ripen, as she expressed it, in the surrounding gloom.

She asked for mineral water, and consommé with an egg in it, and proceeded with her tale.

"Things had been bad with me . . . how, I don't know. . . . They go in cycles, I suppose; for at one time I had, as you know, half the Turf Club . . . how shall I put it . . . on my books?" She made a gesture with her hand, graceful and gracious, to the waiter, who was offering her a dish, and bit her lip and smiled as a man passed in with his wife and daughter, whispering to me, "He is a client," and then coughing a little, began again to talk.

I looked at her with interest, and saw how she had fallen away, that her collar-bones made ridges in her light summer blouse. "Ah yes, I see why you are looking," she said; "it is dreadful to be thin, that is to say, in my line of business, for men seem to like women to be fat, and I am nothing but old bones."

"I think it was a cold I caught coming back from France, where I had been to see my mother. Yes, do not laugh, and please say nothing about *ma mère* for I know you insularies see something comic about that. We, on the other hand, are much more lovers of our family than you, though you think not. Of course, both men and nations always plume themselves on qualities they lack. Yes, I am quite a little of a philosopher, that is, since I was ill. Well, well, it was congestion, as I said, which nailed me to my bed. When you are young and strong and nearly six feet high, as I am," and here she straightened herself up with pride, looking a true descendant of the pirates (she came from Normandy), with her fresh colour, bright grey eyes, and masses of fair hair, "it is silly to be ill. Illness in our profession usually takes us soon to the end of our resources, for we, of course, must make a good appearance, and frequent good restaurants, then we are always robbed by all who deal with us.

"Illness too lifts the veil, or the veneer of chivalry which most of our friends assume to us, although, of course, it also brings what out is good.

"I become a moralist, you see, a dreadful thing in one who has to chatter always and be gay. Ah!" and an ashy look came on her cheeks, "those awful conversations about horses, bad plays, and books, and pictures that you would not use in a back kitchen as a screen. I think the frankly indecent even harasses me less. Your countrymen, you'll pardon me, I know, have little *talent de société*, or perhaps they keep it all for those they think that they respect, that is, if any Englishman really respects a woman in his heart. Chivalry, eh—bah, we see what that means. Either the idea is real, or else it is a fraud. If it is real, it should make a man the same to every woman, especially to us who minister to his pleasures and act as lightning conductors to his home. That sets me thinking"—and here that wintry smile she used as an armour flitted across her face—"why a man's home is to be pure and a woman's not so, for strange as it may seem I have a home, that is a house in which I live. When a man leaves me with his 'Good night, old girl,' I often wonder if he thinks his home is purified by what has taken place in mine. Well, well," and as she drank her coffee, her eyes wandered to the man she knew who, seated with his daughter and his wife, kept his face turned away.

"Yes," she said, "there is a man who, no doubt, in his own home is kind enough, as men are kind, if all goes right with them. You see, I and his daughter, are almost of one age . . . a pretty girl enough she is, and would look better if only she wore good stays. How strange it is, here in this island, you so often see expensive clothes ill-worn and spoiled by villainous bad stays or made ridiculous by a cheap pair of boots, or something of that kind.

"When I fell ill, and when the doctors said I must go home and not live as I had been doing, the father of that girl was one of those to whom I went for help. He never answered when I wrote him, nor for that matter did any of the men who used to like to take me to the theatres when I was well and was a credit to their taste."

She paused and waived away a cigarette, saying she did not want to look like a *bourgeoise en goguette*, and as the man she said she knew walked out behind his women-folk, fixed her eyes on him, till he reddened, as she put it, "at the back of his neck between the collar and the hair."

Then smiling and coughing now and then, she told how one of her friends had pawned her rings to send her home to France and, turning serious, said, "Now I will tell you of a trouble I am in. You know that women of our class, if by some accident we fall in love, love far more fiercely than those that you call honest. I know the Spanish proverb about our love—that it resembles nothing but a fire of straw—but, there, it was concocted by a man . . . *les hommes, ça vous abîme une femme.* Personally I have never felt it . . . that is, but once or twice at most, and each time have regretted it, both for myself and him. You smile when I say 'him,' but it is true. However, that is not now what troubles me, but this.

"I know I cannot follow up this life, nor wish to, and I have told you that it was my ambition to study Art and try and learn to paint. No, no, I do not think I am a genius . . . nothing of the sort, but still I think I might have made a living in the Art world had I but had the chance. Now, though, the thing for me is how to live at all. I think I told you that I was a *mannequin* in a great Paris shop. I am you see both tall and elegant. . . . No, don't laugh . . . it is so; for I was born, although my family was poor, with an innate sense of elegance in dress . . . the sentiment of rags." This was so manifestly true, my friend said nothing, but merely nodded, wondering what she would say. "I cannot go back to that way of life; for during the past years I have lived in luxury, that is to say, I have enjoyed a luxury tempered by the ever-present dread of want, but still a luxury. I have read books and haunted the museums; I know the various schools of painting tolerably well, revel in Corot, adore Degas and Monet, think Whistler inspired, and therefore cannot go home and settle down, marrying some *Betrave* or another, perhaps a local cattle-dealer or something of the sort. Now, though, a chance has come into my life, and I can neither jump at it nor yet neglect it; for as I told you I am *très bonne fille*, and would not like to wreck the life of anyone, especially of one who says he loves me . . . yes, loves me as I am."

She put a falling hairpin back into her hair, played with her bag, taking it up and looking at the clasp. Then put it down and after having sipped her coffee, began again to talk.

"The thing is this way . . I had a lover—a *vieux colonel*, not a bad sort of man, stiff, angular, and with his face reddened by whisky and the sun of India, just such a man as Loti talks about, honourable I think, and wearisome. He liked to spend long hours with me, drinking and telling me about himself, his life, his horses and the women that he thought that he had loved, *cocasse, le Colonel,* but still a gentleman. One day he brought an officer of his to see me. He was, I think, from Lancashire, some kind of a provincial anyway, and above all a type.

"What was he like? Well, short and freckled; such feet and hands, and with a neck the colour of a lobster, with the sun. His clothes not bad, but with a note of something of *le gentilhomme campagnard* about them. For a watch-chain, a leather . . . lip strap, I think, you call the thing . . . it go beneath the curb, and he tell me it is for when the horse shakes his head, so that he cannot turn the bit, and run away with you. Over his boots little white gaiters; and gloves, such gloves—so thick, like the stuff you make a fencing-jacket. Fair hair, what of it was left—not that he was bald, but I mean what the barber he have left—a mouth with teeth like a shark, an eye-glass, and a perpetual transpiration on his skin. Not pleasant-looking, eh? That where you make a mistake, then. He did look pleasant, and a gentleman, although he never said a word but 'Aoh yes, awful pleased to meet yer,' with an occasional 'Ha,' which at first made me jump.

"Why the colonel brought him I never could make out, but from the first night I saw his junior officer had fallen in love with me.

"I am not as a rule nervous . . . well . . . under fire; but this man, his very bashfulness made me feel like a milk-maid when her lover sits upon a gate and whistles at her. Not a word did he say whilst his superior officer imbibed champagne, and talked of horses he had known thirty or forty years ago, except to interject a 'Ha' at intervals. At last, though, it seemed near ending, the colonel rose to go. He pulled me to him, and giving me a winy kiss or two, remarked: 'Good-bye, old girl, we're going now. Ta! ta! Be virtuous and you'll be unhappy,' or something of the kind.

"I turned and saw to my amazement that the lieutenant, who had drunk little, that is for one of his great bulk, had turned quite pale, and glared with rage at his commanding officer.

"He let his eyeglass fall with a loud chink against his waistcoat buttons, and holding out his hand said: 'Good-bye, some day I'll call again'; so like a gentleman I—I own, was surprised.

"After a day or two I got a letter from him—not too well written, and with a fault or two in the orthography—saying he meant to come and see me to-morrow afternoon.

"Of course I thought it was the usual kind of thing, and when the time came dressed myself in a light peignoir, laced, and with views to the inside, as we say. It suited me, fair as I am, and with my yellow hair, for it was colour *eau de Nil*, and as the gladiators when they marched round the ring no doubt put on their best, I always like to look my best when I expect to be a sacrifice.

"Punctually at the time he said, my officer came in. I came to meet him, smiling, thinking perhaps that he would kiss me, after the fashion of his kind, who do not generally waste time in words or in preliminaries. However, he held out his hand, and said a little stiffly: 'Glad to see you looking well,' and sitting down upon a chair, began to look at me. What an original, I thought, as he kept staring at me, until I half began to blush with his continued gaze.

"His eyes roved round the room, and now and then his monocle fell, and he would put it back again, with a contortion of his face, like something on the stage.

"At last he fixed his eyes upon a picture that I had . . . well, *un peu leste*, but nothing very shocking, and turning red, he pointed up at it, observing: 'What a beastly thing. Ha! yes, abominable.' I did not know if I should laugh or be angry, but going to it, turned it round against the wall and said: 'Now are you satisfied?' Then with some difficulty and with a number of 'Ha's' to help him through his tale, he said he loved me. I had not heard a man say that for the last five years, and it took me by surprise, so I said nothing, and I think turned red a little. Still I did not take in his meaning, and made a motion as of rising, for I expected he was like the rest of them. 'Not that,' he said. 'By God! Ha! No, I really mean it. Miss Elise, I love you awfully.'

"Still I said nothing, for what on earth was there to say." After a little while he went away, but came again at intervals, always the same—stiff, red and awkward, and with the same song on his lips.

"At last one day, quite *à brûle-pourpoint*, he asked me would I marry him, but quite respectfully, and in a way that rather made me like him . . . it was phenomenal. What could I say, especially as after saying what he had he took my hand and looking at me through his monocle said: 'Could you love a fellow?'

"I was sore put to it, for I saw that I had to do with quite another sort of monsieur to him I told you of before.

"Love and my officer were not to be carried in one bag. Well, I felt grateful to him, for I understood the sacrifice he was prepared to make far better than he did himself, poor innocent.

"When he had pressed me for an answer, I told him all that he would have to undergo if I said 'Yes' to him. His horses—I had not told you he was in the cavalry—would all have to be sold. He gulped a little comically, for he was a great polo player, but manfully agreed. As his own colonel knew me, he would have to change into another regiment. . . . I thought of foot. . . . Of course I had to do the thinking . . . and go to India. He said that it would be a wrench, and that the Grabbies were a beastly lot. However, he would do it all, if I would love a fellow.

"As he talked on and held my hand, at first half timidly and then as in a vice, I rather liked him: he was so childlike and original; but an original.

"Love—no, that was impossible, and so I told him. His

face fell for a minute, but he returned again, back to the charge. He didn't care. Ha! no, not a bit. I was the only woman that he ever cared for, and if I only would consider, take time, er—he did not wish to hurry me . . . so like a gentleman."

Elise stopped for a moment and then——

"I have taken time to think of it, and cross to-night to France, paying my passage with the money that my friend pawned her rings to get for me. His money I refused to take. . . . I, too, have honour . . . and the best thing for me is to go home to my own village Pont de l'Evêque, and try and get my health.

"Then I shall live *en paysanne*, go to bed early, and in the morning hear the swallows in the roof; there used to be a nest above my window three or four years ago. How good their morals are compared to ours . . . I mean the swallows. 'Tis quite an idyll to see them feed their young ones, and the male never looks at any bird, except his *légitime*.

"When I feel better I shall go to Mass, not that I am a firm believer, still less a practiser, but the thing does you good somehow—perhaps the singing, or perhaps the recollection of one's childhood, or something of the kind.

"So I am off, and in a day or two shall be perhaps wandering along the Chaussée, with its double rows of trees, silvery, and looking like a Corot against the fields of corn.

"I shall be thinking of what I told you, and of how difficult it is to love a fellow. Then, when I am better, who knows what I shall do? . . . Ah! *méchant*. No, never, I swear it; he said he never would till we were married . . : you see he was not in the least like you, or any other man."

SIGNALLED

THE Casino rooms were crowded. French, English, Poles, Russians and an occasional Japanese, looking just like a monkey who had escaped from freedom in the woods and voluntarily had put the chains of trousers and of coats about his limbs, all jostled in the throng. Above them hung the concentrated scent of all the perspirations of their different races, mingled with every essence that the perfumer's art affords to mitigate the odours which humanity distils. All were well dressed, and eighteen centuries of culture and of care had culminated in making every one alike. Thus all spoke French, of course with varying accents; but as they all read the same books, had the same thoughts, and wore the selfsame clothes, the accident of accent did not separate them, and they formed one immense, well-scented family as to exteriors, though with their hands all secretly raised against each other, and their tongues wagging ceaselessly in calumny, just as a bulrush wags by the edge of some old mill-race, half filled up with mud.

All round the tables men and women stood, pushing and elbowing, and with their eyes fixed on the money on the cloth, adoringly, as it had been the Holy Grail and they all vowed to search for and to grasp it, at the peril of their souls.

Men who at home were magistrates and pillars of a church, or members of some county council, gazed at the demi-mondaines as they went to and fro brushing against the players to attract attention, with their eyes aflame or with a swinish puckering of their lips which spoke of lust unsatisfied, not from religious principles, but from the fear of spies and interfering friends.

They eyed the women just as a starving dog looks at a

butcher's shop, sideways and lurkingly, for fear a blow may fall upon him, out of some quarter unforeseen. Smartly dressed women looked at their sisters of the demi-monde half with dislike half with approval, as if they somehow understood that they, although they were transgressors of trades-union rules, were helping them in their life's strife with man; whilst others with the colour rising in their cheeks pressed up against them as they passed, just as cats press against a chair, meeting their eyes with a bold comprehending stare. Remote from all the rest in a cane rocking-chair there sat a girl, thin, dark and dressed quite quietly, so quietly that at first sight you might have taken her for a young married woman who had got separated from her friends and had sat down to rest.

Her high-heeled shoes just tapped upon the ground as the chair rocked, and as it balanced to and fro revealed her stockings half way up the calf, so fine and worked so open, that it appeared the hair upon the flesh might pass between the stitching, just as a little fish escapes through the fine meshes of a net.

Men passed before her, in the half-sneaking and half-swaggering way that men assume before a woman whom they have held between their arms a night or two ago, and whom they dare not recognize in public, although they want the world to see that they are well acquainted, and in its censure half applaud the fact. Their hands involuntarily just touched their hats, and as they looked an inch or two above her head murmured a greeting, and then straightening their legs they fell into a strut, as of a bull-fighter who has been nearly caught by the bull's horns, and wants the crowd to think he is not frightened as he edges to the limits of the ring. She gave her salutation by a half rising of her eyebrows, and a faint smile, half of amusement and half contempt, just flickered on her lips, as some one with his wife or daughter on his arm suddenly flushed or paled and looked with interest at the chandelier as he passed opposite her chair. Callow and fledgling youths boldly saluted her, colouring as they did so to their hair, whilst grave and decorated men just raised their eyes, and fat provincials wildly plunged and bolted at the sight of her, just like young horses faced suddenly in a deep lane by the fierce rattle of a motor-car.

Still nothing in her dress or manner was unlike that of a hundred other women in the rooms, as she sat quietly at the receipt of custom, watching her various acquaintances as they passed by give by their guilty looks the lie both to the faith and the morality they held, and which no doubt she held herself as sacred, and as fixed as are the poles, although she saw them outraged in her person twenty times a week, just as in Spain, 'tis said, that a society founded to protect the lower animals, finding itself in difficulties, arranged a bull-fight to increase its funds and clear away its debts.

But as she sat indifferent, waiting what fate should send her, to her amazement another girl, but little younger than herself, sat down beside her, and with "Il fait tray sho nais-ce pars," fell into conversation with her as easily as if they had been friends.

The girl who knew the world glanced at her quickly, half thinking that the stranger came from some island in the Ægean Sea, but saw at once her island lay to the north, and that she had addressed her in pure innocence of heart.

Though she had often seen fair English girls, dressed in short skirts, boisterous in manner, fresh-coloured and half manlike in their ways, striding along as if their knees would burst their petticoats, this was the first time she had met or spoken to one, and the experience somehow brought the blood into her cheeks.

"Yes, it is hot," she said, and stole a glance half of amazement, half approbation, at the fresh English girl, who seated by her side seemed quite unconscious of the difference in their lives and talked so naturally and in such curious French. She marked her sunburned hands, gloveless and strong as those of a young man, and, made observant by the manner of her life, saw she was pretty at a glance, although her clothes were ugly and her fair hair all gathered in a knot. As she thought upon this thing and on that, and on the shielded life of the fair English girl, so little younger than herself, and on her own, a flush rose on her face as she perceived that she was shy before the other's innocence and want of knowledge of the world. At first the conversation languished, till the stranger, who had sat down with so much lack of ceremony beside her, looking her over with wide-open eyes, said: "I liked the look of you, as I was straying up and down, looking out for my mother, who had got lost whilst I was watching the roulette. You looked so pretty, and you are well dressed, you know you are, and so does everyone; all the men look at you, when they pass by, just as a schoolboy at a cake in a shop-window. How foolish they all are."

Used to all kinds of compliments point-blank, none that she ever had received, in all her life, had put her to such difficulty, and once again she stole a look at her fair complimenter's face to reassure herself that she was really as innocent as she appeared to be. "Well dressed," she murmured; "well, any woman likes to be well dressed." To such a commonplace of femininity no answer was required beyond a simple affirmation, and a look of admiration at the clothes.

"Why, what a lot of men you know!" the English girl exclaimed, as counts and viscounts whom she knew by name walked by, as they sat talking, staring a little at the strange companionship of the two girls, all making a half recognition as they passed. "Why is it, none of them take off their hats—I thought that Frenchmen always were polite?"

Then as she got no answer, but a tapping of her companion's heels upon the floor, and a faint blush as of annoyance at her words, fearing she had offended her acquaintance, whom she already had begun to admire on account of her nice clothes, and evident knowledge of the world, she said, just as a schoolboy might have said: "It's awful hot in here.

Would you mind going out into the air and we can sit and talk?" The other, like a person in a dream, got up and followed her, and the two girls walked through the crowd, the English girl quite unconcerned, pushing her way, after the fashion of a forward player in a football team, smiling and only anxious to get out into the air. The other, red and uncomfortable, but hypnotized by the frank manners and good faith of her she followed, hardly knew where she was until she found herself seated in a cane chair upon the terrace, and heard her guide say: "Well, this is better than the stuffy room."

From the Casino came the hum of voices, and points of light seemed to break through the windows, and a faint smell of perspiration and stale scent defiled the atmosphere as it came floating up to where they sat. A breeze sprang up and cleared away the fleecy clouds before the moon, whose rays, half deadened by the glare of the electric lamps upon the terrace, seemed to be concentrated shyly on the magnolia trees which formed the background of the artificial scene, falling on their metallic-looking leaves, which it subdued and turned to plates of silver in its light. Moths hung about the great electric lamps, like men about a courtesan, and seemed to swim in the long beam of light which issued from the globes. Sometimes they flew against the glass with a dull furry noise, and then fell stunned and lay upon the paths, with their wings fluttering, until some high-heeled shoe, just peeping out from underneath a cataract of lace, crushed them to pulp upon the stones, or carried off their bodies sticking to the sole.

Silence fell on the girls as, walking to the balustrade, they stood and looked over the wide white road, across the lawn set with its bunches of white pampas-grass and of euonymus, upon the sea, which stretched out cool and clean and undefiled even by all the tawdriness of the Casino and its lights. Up from the shore there came a long-drawn sigh as if the waves had brought to land the last expiring breath of some lost sailor as they swirled upon the beach. The light air stirred the curls upon the foreheads of the girls, and the mysterious companionship of youth drew them together without words making them feel a bond of sympathy.

Tears stood in the dark eyes of the French girl, she did not quite know why, and something seemed to force her to bestow her confidence upon the girl who stood beside her, although she felt it would be useless, as she could never understand.

As she stood hesitating, the other, seeing her tears, caught at her hands and said: "I say, whatever is the matter? I am so sorry. Tell us about it, it will do you good, Is it about any of those bounders who grinned at you, and did not raise their hats?"

The other looked at her, and struggling to keep back her tears, said: "No, no, not about any man, I hate them all . . . that is, I am not sure . . . I think one is not quite so horrible as all the rest—but then I have no right to talk to you, so innocent, about such things." She felt the hand of her companion tighten on her own, and all her sorrows running from her heart; her prostituted youth, the recollection of her home, perhaps the thought of the one man less horrible than were the others, forced her to speak and lay her head upon the shoulder of the mysterious friend, who had come as it were out of the depths to comfort her.

As she was struggling to choke down her tears and speak, and as the English girl stood wondering, but sympathetic and expectant, clasping her hands in hers, a strong high voice broke through the stillness of the night.

"Ethel, my dear," it said, "where have you got to? We have been looking for you for the last hour, and father is so cross." The girls just pressed each other's hands and separated, as ships which have but signalled may be parted by a mist, without the time to make out either their numbers or the ports from which they hail.

WRIT IN SAND

AT sundown long lines of motor vans, as huge as arks, converged upon a sandy waste space of the southern little town. Over it towered the Ligurian Alps, rugged and sun-scorched. The waves of Mare Nostrum just lapped against the sea wall that bounded the neglected piece of ground on which a canvas city was to arise, like Jonah's gourd, during the night. The vans scrunched on the pebbles as they came up in long procession, and formed a great corral.

Each monstrous car took its own place with mathematical precision, for Amar's Circus had been long upon the road, having pushed what it called upon its posters "Une Audacieuse Randonnée" as far as Angora, and was now back again in France.

From the cars came the cries of animals, the miauling of the lions, the grunts of camels, and the stamping of the horses eager to be fed.

The scent that can be best described as "Bouquet de Cirque," compounded of the odours of the various animals, sawdust and orange peel, of petrol, dried perspiration, leather, of cordage, canvas ill laid up when damp, cheap perfumes and cosmetics, all the quintessence of a world apart from any other kind of world, a world where men and women risk their lives daily, and reck nothing of it, a world in which they live, in fellowship with horses, elephants and mules, a fellowship that makes them different to all other kind of men, as sailors were in the old world of wind-jammers, floated out into the night air. An army sprang into existence, as it were, from the ground, composed of workmen, unlike any other workmen, looking for the most part like grooms and chauffeurs out of place, but smart, alert and singularly quick upon their feet. All of them seemed able to turn a somersault, saddle a horse, or swarm up a rope ladder, as well as a smart seaman in an old China tea clipper, when he ran aloft into a top, over the futtock shrouds. Babel itself, when Jahwe, out of jealousy of man set confusion on the tongue of men, was not more polyglot. Russian, American, English, French, Italian, Spanish, Arabic, German, and Czechoslovak jostled one another in their mouths. None spoke the others' language properly, but everyone knew the word for horse, rope, saddle, dance, sawdust, knot, slack or tight wire, handspring and elephant, in the others' tongue. For ordinary purposes, they had formed a lingua franca, out of the various elements of speech of all the languages, shotted with oaths and with indecencies, that worn as smooth as pebbles in the current of their speech had become merely adjectives.

These heterogeneous good companions, for no one better merited the term, like ants, set at once busily to work, under the blue glare of the electric light, that as by magic, others of the band had installed on what an hour ago was a mere sandy waste.

Long tents, to serve as stables, grew up like mushrooms, leaving a vacant space, where the great tent should rise. To them, men in trousers of a horsy cut, or breeches unbuttoned at the knees, muffled in greatcoats with woollen comforters up to their ears, covering their gipsy-looking greasy hair, for far Multan had sent its quota to the kaleidoscopic host, led horses that stepped as quietly and unconcernedly as if the planks down which they walked had been green fields, those fields that they would see no more, for once a circus horse their lot is fixed as the fixed stars.

Piebalds, roans, chestnuts, sorrels, duns, skewbalds, creams with black points, steel-greys, and whites of every shade from purest snow to honey-coloured and that palest shade of cream, known in the Argentine as Duck's Egg, formed an equine flower-bed.

Chiron himself when seated underneath a spreading oak in Thessaly—he chose the finest of the mares to blend with

the most beautiful of the young men to form the Centaur,
that flight of man's imagination, that for once has outgone
nature—could not have found better material to his hand.
The equine race of the whole world has furnished representa-
tives, from Shetland ponies up to the heavy Mecklenburger,
with his round back, fit to count money on, and his stout
legs, that do not seem to feel the strain when six or seven
riders poise and caper on him as he canters round the ring.
Yukers from the Hungarian puzta, with their fine limbs,
light bone and saddle backs, as if nature itself had formed
them for the circus, intelligent and docile, their long and
flowing manes and tails, full gentle eyes and open nostrils
giving them the look of an Arabian steed designed in tapestry
upon a banner screen in a Victorian house. In a long line
they stepped out of their boxes, as delicately as Agag, with
that look of comprehension and disdain performing animals
all acquire, as if they felt the difference between an artist and
a mere spectator, lolling in his stall, with a fat paunch and
well-filled pocket-book.

After the horses had disappeared into their stables, a drove
of camels, herded by Algerians, or Moroccans, but perhaps
best described as "natives," for in what lone duar, or in
what black tent of camels' hair they had first heard the call to
prayers, only themselves and Allah could pronounce with
certainty.

Dressed in brown jellabas, or dingy white burnouses, they
yet preserved entire their racial look, that almost all the other
members of the troupe had shed when they took on their
circensian nationality.

When the lions, tigers, seals and all the other wild beasts
that made the now rapidly growing canvas town look as if
Noah's Ark was delivering her cargo on Mount Ararat,
had been caged, slowly the elephant appeared, with the look
of peculiar cunning in his little porcine eyes that makes him
only just inferior to mankind, as to intelligence, although
perhaps superior in bonhomie. He seemed to feel the dignity

of his position as a survivor of a prehistoric world. All the time that the animals were being settled in their stables, the work went on, but silently, so that when a great canvas dome slowly was hoisted into position in the middle of the waste piece of ground, it seemed to rise out of its own volition from the sand. Then and then only was the noise of hammers heard, as a platoon of men drove home great iron tent pegs, to tauten up the ropes.

Around the ring they ranged the padded barrier, fencing in its thirteen paces of diameter, that sacramental measurement in which horses and men perform in circuses, all the world over, whether in the centre of great cities or in a field outside a village, in rural England, Poland or Hungary. Seats, boxes, and electric lights, the high trapezes swinging from the roof, appeared to have been always just where the efficient squads of workers had placed them only half an hour before.

By daybreak all was ready for the next day's performance, and when the ring-master, wrapped in an old, white box-cloth greatcoat with huge bone buttons, and a woollen comforter round his neck, looked at the work, and said, like the great ring-master in Eden, "that it was good," a hoot on an electric whistle summoned all hands to breakfast in the dining tent.

In the real, or the unreal world, according to the point of view of those who live in, or outside, a circus, the false dawn had vanished, and the sun was rising over the mountains and the sea. A white mist hung upon the palm trees, magnifying and ennobling them, just as it does out in the desert, or in the tropic everglades, from whence they had originally been brought. The sun's first rays fell on the lateen sails of the fishing boats as they stole out from every little village port and launched into the sea. From them there came the muffled sounds of oars, of cordage creaking in the old-time wooden blocks, as the great yard, that Latin yard, common to all the boats that sail the Latin sea was hoisted into place. Such yards, and ships not much unlike the fishing boats that now began to feel the morning breeze, the ships of Agamemnon and Ulysses, must have borne when Helen's smile launched them upon the siege of Troy. The fishing boats, their pointed sails giving them an air as of a flight of seabirds, sank by degrees below the horizon, as silently as gulls disappear into the haze, before the eye of man can mark their disappearance. Shoreward, the rippling waves lapped on the pebbly beaches, with a scrunching sound as of the cat-ice crackling on the edges of a pond.

The ragged mountains, dotted with villages grouped round their church, the houses sheltering about it, as it were for protection from the modern world, just caught the morning sun. The panorama, fantastic and unreal, with the white houses of the coastal towns, the imported vegetation, and their look of unreality, seemed designed as an ideal background for the great dome of canvas that billowed gently, shivering a little in the light sea breeze, just as a jellyfish thrown up by the sea shivers upon the sand.

All was in order, by the hour advertised. A van with windows cut at intervals, behind which sat well-dressed girls, as quiet and orderly as typists in a city office, served as the box-office. All seemed as permanent as if the dome of canvas had been the dome of a cathedral, stone-built and pointed, designed to last for centuries. Nothing about it gave an air of instability, but set one thinking that in a fleeting world, where all is changing (but as invisibly as the hands move upon a clock), canvas is the most fit material to build with, for those whose lives are after all passed in a circus, where they perform, even with less volition of their own than the trained animals, and pass away as the smoke of a cigarette dissolves into the air.

Bands blared, and men standing before the side-shows shouted the charms of the bearded lady, pig with five legs, the human skeleton, and the fat women from Trebizond, certain of custom, for mankind unaware of its own freakishness, delights in abnormalities, seeing in them perhaps, something they can wonder at, despise, and patronise, and leave the tent amused and comforted by their superiority.

A continuous stream of people passed the wicket gate where stood the gigantic negro in a green uniform, with that grin upon his face that makes the people of his race quite as inscrutable as the most enigmatic Japanese or Chinaman. Packed close as sardines in a barrel, the audience had that air of expectation that circus audiences must have manifested since the time of the Romans and the Greeks.

In the reserve seats sat a few tourists, some beautifully dressed in plus-fours, that costume tailors have designed as in derision of humanity. The well-known smell of tan, of horses' urine and of orange peel, with all the various scents, human and those compounded by perfumers, that every audience in the world throws off, luckily unknown to itself, hung in the air, in spite of all the efforts of smartly-dressed attendants, who wielded sprinklers with disinfectants.

Gone were the days when everything was dingy, the coats of horses staring, the performers' dresses dirty or ill-washed. All was as spick and span as in a West-End theatre. Smart girls in velvet coats of Georgian cut, flowered waistcoats, knee-breeches and silk stockings, high-heeled shoes, leaving a train of scent in passing, sold programmes and showed people to their seats, with an air fit for any court, or at least such courts as those of Monaco and Gerolstein. The seats, the boxes and the ring itself were models of neatness and of cleanliness, and that, although the circus had been upon the road for months, travelling in Asia Minor and in Turkey, and only meant to spend three days where they had pitched their tents, and take the road again.

Into the arena bounded a Hungarian horse "en liberté," dark chestnut, with white stockings and a blaze down its face that made it "drink in white," as the Brazilians say.

Coursing round the ring, it seemed to cover miles, although the whole circumference was but a hundred feet. At a sign from the ringmaster, who, dressed in evening clothes, his chambrière with the lash lying on the ground, the fiery courser of the desert (see the handbills) stopped and reversed its course. Then, rising on its hind legs, it fought the air before the whirling lash that never touched it, and following its trainer, to the opening in the barrier, bounded back to its stables, passing through the ranks of the attendants, in their green uniforms, who clapped it on the quarters as it passed.

Men and girls rode, springing from the ground on to their horses' backs as agilely as gauchos. They faced the tail, balanced themselves on one another's shoulders, straddled their horses' necks, and passed beneath their bellies coming up on the other side, vaulted over the hind quarters, were dragged round the arena holding to the tail, whilst all the time the docile animals galloped like clockwork, as if they knew their riders' limbs were in their care, and that as much depended on them as on the men and women in their partnership.

A Caucasian horseman galloped into the ring. About the middle height, handsome and as "wonderly deliver" as was the Knight of the Canterbury Tales, the Caucasian dress suited him to perfection. The long green, fur-trimmed coat, set with its silver cartridge cases on the breast, clung to a waist as slender as a girl's, the red, soft, heelless riding boots, that eastern horsemen all affect, were home into the stirrups, that with their short leathers did not allow the feet to come below the belly, and gave the rider the appearance of standing upright on his horse, in the big peaked Cossack saddle with its pads, like footballs, that support the thighs. You saw at once that he was a Gigit, trained to the tricks of the best school of Gigitofka, in Vladikafkas, or some other mountain town in the recesses of the frosty Caucasus. His Persian lambswool cap, set off his bold and sun-browned features, leaving a few tight curls below it, on his forehead. His light and cutting snaffle bridle, with its thin red reins, he held high, in his left hand, to give a better purchase on the palate, for the Caucasian horsemen use no curb. Holding one hand above his head, his nagaika dangling from his forefinger, he rushed into the arena checking his Anglo-Arab in the centre of the ring, where it stood, turned to stone, for half a second, before he wheeled it once again into full speed. Rising in his short stirrups he stood erect upon the saddle, and then letting himself fall trailed round the ring with his head just brushing on the sand. Agile as a cat, he swung himself again into his seat, threw down a handkerchief, retrieved it from the saddle, with a "back pick-up," and riding gently round the ring, amid thunders of applause, saluted gravely with his hand touching his lambswool cap.

The women looked at him, as if he were a cake in a con fectioner's, devouring him in anticipation with their eyes. Some said he was a prince in his own country, which may have been the case, for certainly he looked a prince upon his horse. Well did Cervantes say that riding makes some men appear like grooms, others like princes.

Next appeared a troupe of Chinese acrobats; modern Chinese without their pigtails, who had travelled the world over and spoke every language, and yet the instant that they set saucers spinning on a long slender cane, or piled a line of rods on one another, striking away the lowest of the pile and deftly catching the topmost rod upon one finger-point, became as oriental and inscrutable as if they had never left their native country for an hour. Even in the circus ring they seemed to represent a culture that had existed centuries before Europe had emerged from barbarism.

More graceful if less powerful than their Western brethren, who with their great muscles looked a little crude beside them, they seemed as if their feats were an hieratic ritual from an older world, rather than circus tricks. On her bay thorough-bred, with patterns traced upon its quarters with dandy brush and water, his coat so bright and shining that a man could shave by it, the lady of the Haute Ecole rode gracefully into the ring. Seated in her white buckskin saddle, she held her reins so lightly that they scarcely seemed to move, but with a grip as strong as steel. The smartly fitting habit showed her well-cut patent-leather boot, set off with a bright spur. Holding her long Haute Ecole whip in her right hand, she touched her horse upon the shoulder gently, putting him through all the airs of the manège, the Spanish Walk, the Passage, Volte and Semivolte, making him shift his croup, change feet with his hind legs, rear, plunge and finally kneel down, whilst she leaned back in the saddle easily, smiling her thanks to the delighted audience. The ring-master, advancing, held her horse as she dismounted at a bound, and bowing to the audience, retired, executing two or three of those little skips without which no feminine performer in a circus ever leaves the ring. Demos must have his jesters just as in older ages emperors and kings kept private fools at courts. In this age of mass production the clowns who have replaced, or perhaps merely succeeded, the jesters of an older world, for nothing changes in man's mental atmosphere, tumbled by platoons into the ring. Their antics, quips, quiddities and cranks fell rather flat on a French public, too civilised and not attuned to "le gros rire" that so delights a British audience. Perhaps the national lack of bonhomie accounts for it to some extent, but certainly jokes that set audiences in other countries hilarious with delight, were received rather coldly, much in the way one listens to the club bore with his well-worn and pointless platitudes.

One turn and only one the clowns apparently held in reserve for all eventualities fairly brought down the house, and dissipated the air of cold reserve and condescension that their first efforts had not availed to thaw.

Dressed as a comic Spanish bull-fighter, mimicking the airs of a Matamoros that bull-fighters affect, hollowing his back and strutting, whilst he held his wooden sword in the approved position, over the red cloak doubled on his left arm, a tall thin clown advanced into the ring. Stopping before a pretty girl, perhaps placed there by the ring-master in the same way that company promoters get a mine "salted" before they give the public the privilege of purchasing their shares, he laid his hand upon his heart, made a mock heroic speech, and with the appropriate gesture flung his "montera" on the ground. Then from the entrance rushed in a great dog, equipped with horns, and hunted him after a few ineffectual passes, all round the ring. Dropping his wooden sword and all his airs of a Torero, the clown rushed about in unavailing efforts to escape the onslaughts of the "bull." At last he fairly fled before his adversary, who seized him by the collar of his jacket and was borne out struggling, behind the scenes. Then for the first time the audience gave itself up to the magnetism that once started surely affects a crowd, and laughed till tears ran down the rough faces of the peasants from the villages and made respectable and well-dressed bourgeois shake their fat sides with laughter, and wipe their glasses as they leaned back in their seats, vanquished by that one touch of folly that makes the whole world kin. No circus is complete nowadays without its "drug store" cowboys to spin a rope and ride a horse trained to plunge three or four times, without putting up its back, that the audience takes to be a buckjumper. They may or may not have been real cowpunchers, once upon a time, but generally come from some western cow-town, where they have learned to lasso in the local stockyards and corrals. They wore silk shirts, wristlets of patent leather, and round their necks gaudy silk handkerchiefs, artistically knotted, that fell upon their shoulders in two points, forming what is called a golilla by the Mexicans, though the word, no doubt brought over by the Conquistadores, really means a ruff. Their loose, rather low riding boots, slashed in the front with red and yellow leather, were stuffed into their trousers, cut tightly, such as the Mexicans affect. Each of them carried a well-coiled lasso in his hands. With wonderful dexterity, they spun their lassos, forming the loop so quickly it seemed a living thing that grew beneath their hands. Gradually it circled up and down, rising and falling round the body of the lassoer, who jumped through the loop, threw a back somersault, lay down and rose again, till finally the fifty feet of the long heavy rope, in a vast ring, was whirling in the air. The other youth spun a rope in each hand, keeping a short cord spinning in his teeth. He cracked a stockwhip, cutting a piece of paper from his companion's hands, at ten or twelve feet off, a feat that would have cost a finger-joint to the man who held the piece of paper had the lash fallen upon it.

Then a man stood against a shutter, with his arms extended, and the two youths outlined his figure on the boards with butchers' knives, thrown with such force they quivered in the wood.

Nothing appeared to interest the audience so much, for it was something anyone could understand, with the additional element of danger to another's life, so dear to those who pass their own removed from any risk. For the first time the faces of the youths took on a grave expression, and as they drew the knives out of the shutter one whispered something to the other, who, glancing for a moment over his shoulder, smiled and spat upon the ground. Then came the turn that showed the difference between circus tricks, however dexterous, and roping on a ranch. In the one case a man depends upon himself, and as a juggler by continual practice performs feats that appear incredible, so does the circus lasso expert make a rope seem almost living in his deft hands. Upon a ranch, or even in a circus, to rope animals is quite another matter, for it is impossible to train a horse into co-operation with the man who wields the rope. All that can be done by the best trainer in the world is to ensure that the horse gallops evenly and does not flinch when the man makes his cast. The knife-throwing over, and the trained buckjumper duly ridden, a man in chaparreras, a word the cow-punchers have changed to "chaps," wearing a ten-gallon hat, and all the rest of the indumentaria of his calling, rode into the ring.

He put his horse into a slow canter, bearing a little on the bit to make him raise his forehand, whilst the roper, watching his opportunity, stood by to throw and catch the horse by the front feet. He dwelt a little long upon his aim, perhaps through over-care, and as he threw his cast was just a fraction of a second late, and struck the horse's legs as they touched ground, instead of circling them when in the air. The rope came back into his hand, like a snake recoils upon itself if it has missed its spring—a most annoying thing to happen to a man who knows that he knows how to rope, but that occasionally occurs to the best cattlemen.

His companion muttered something to him that made him frown, and gathering up his lasso after a sign to the man upon the horse, he poised himself again to throw his rope.

This time he tried to do the feat a little differently. Instead of aiming at the forelegs, when in the air, he threw the loop in front of them, intending that the horse should step into the noose, and with a deft twist of his wrist to pull it up upon the legs. Again he was a trifle soon, and only caught one foot, an ugly throw that pulls the limb out in an ungainly position, and in the case of a wild animal may cause an accident.

The audience not knowing anything about such matters cheered vociferously. Honour was saved, and the two youths retired, dragging their legs a little, with the gait, real or assumed, of men who pass their lives trailing great spurs upon their feet.

No one can tell why the European who generally acts as a mahout to a trained elephant should always be got up as a French explorer in an old-fashioned book of travels, in spotless white, with a sun helmet on his head. Yet so it is, and as the elephant is a discerning animal, it may be that he would not perform if his mahout adopted any other costume. Elephants have performed in circuses ever since the times of ancient Rome, when they walked upon the tight rope, danced, fought in the arena, and perhaps now and then knelt on a

Christian, when Nero was in search of novelty.

Educated, or rather civilised spectators—the two states are not identical—must always look with compassion on a performing elephant. Certainly he is not overworked, but somehow he strikes one as though he would be more in his own element piling great logs into position in a teak forest in Burmah, or helping to make roads in Southern India.

To see the monster, with his intelligence, and his docility, so careful not to hurt any of the pygmies, fussing about him, is a sad sight, and sympathy goes out to the elephant. When the mahout orders him to lie down, it is as if the dignity of man, a dignity, if he is worthy of it, that he should share with all the animals, is being outraged. Standing on a tub, it is as if a valued friend was put into the pillory for fools to gape at. When the mahout swings himself upon his head by one of his tremendous ears, and strikes an attitude as if he were defying the stage thunder, it shows at once that there must be some kind of partnership between the man and the huge animal.

But when the trainer makes him stand up, balancing himself on his forelegs, it is a sight as sorry as it would be to see a learned judge, duly bewigged and robed, after delivering his judgment in an important case, turn round and elevate his worshipful posterior in the air for the inspection of the people seated in the court. He waddled off, with his mahout cracking a whip, to stand and muse perhaps in his own quarters on the strange ways of men, or to be wrapped in the contemplation of his travels from the time when, as a calf, he first set out, following his mother, to be a wanderer upon the road. The pity of it is that he cannot write memoirs, for if he could, how many things he might be able to impart about ourselves, that have escaped our eyes!

The cruel spectacle over, cruel, that is, to those who feel that elephants were not intended to be clowns, for without doubt his trainer loved him as the apple of his eye, addressing him in private life as "mon vieux," "old fellow," or "viejito,"

according to his nationality, and would have braved the flames
to save him had the circus taken fire, four bay horses trotted
into the ring.

Standing in the centre of the arena, much in the way a
hostess in an embassy stands to receive her guests, the ring-
master, in immaculate dress-clothes, stood to receive them
on their entry. They bowed their heads, pawed gently with
their near forefeet, and waited his commands. All were in
high condition, with their coats shining, as bright as a horse-
chestnut, when in the autumn it falls and bursts its covering
on the green moss beneath the trees; their eyes were bright,
their manes and tails well combed and dandy-brushed, their
feet polished like new cricket-balls, and all were so alike that
the best ranchman accustomed to pick out a single horse
from amongst hundreds running in a corral might have been
puzzled to say which, in the language of his craft, was which,
and which the other of them.

At a sign from the ring-master, they ranged themselves
like soldiers, and cantered round the ring, and as they passed
the opening to the stables, four greys joined them, and then
four chestnuts, and four blacks. All were as well matched
and as well turned out as the first four, and as they galloped
they went so evenly and were in such condition that you
might have counted money on their backs without a single
piece of it falling to the ground. They wheeled and stopped,
changed front, and strung out into a long line, put their feet
on the barrier, and came back again into their formation, like
well-regulated clockwork. All seemed to take a pride in their
own beauty, and a pleasure in their work, and now and then
in passing, nipped at each other playfully, or threw up their
heels as they fell into line.

Taking their trainer as a pivot, at a walk they formed a
cartwheel and revolved slowly, the various colours serving
as the spokes.

Lastly the trainer raised his chambrière and whirling it
about before their noses, they rose on their hind legs, fighting

the air with their forefeet, so close to him that he seemed to disappear, lost in the thicket of their flowing manes and tails, with their feet flashing round his head.

He lowered his whip, and forming fours again, they trotted off, each four waiting decorously till it received the signal to advance towards the opening. Then the attendants raked the ring where the horses' feet had churned it up, till it looked like a little sandhill in the desert, after a troup of camels has passed over it. As one of them unhooked the rope-ladder that dangled from the roof, all heads were turned towards a little platform at the end of the tight wire that stretched high above the ring. Balancing poles were fastened to it, and a white wooden chair. From the back there appeared three figures wrapped in greatcoats, whom hardly anyone had seen enter, as everyone had his eyes fixed upon the wire. "The Perestrello Family, the greatest wire-walkers the world has ever seen, renowned for their amazing feats, that have called forth the admiration of all beholders in both hemispheres"; so said the programme, now advanced, shedding their wrappers, to where the ladder hung.

A hum of admiration greeted them when they stood ready to perform, for Latin audiences have never lost their love of beauty in the human form, that has come down to them from their ancestors in Rome, who in their turn received it from the Greeks.

Just for an instant the trio remained motionless, feeling the pride instinctively of their appearance, just as a fine horse appears to feel and to rejoice in his condition, and as unconsciously. With his arms thrown round his children's waists the father looked at them with that air of love and of possession that a fond father feels in something that he has given life to. In this case not only had he given life, but doubly created, by his care in training up to physical perfection those copies of himself.

Not more than five-and-forty years of age, and about five-feet-eight in height, the ideal stature for a perfect athlete of the ring, his crisp brown hair curled low upon his forehead, as the Greeks have depicted in their statues of Olympian victors. His muscles stood out on his arms, but not so much as to amount to a deformity, as is so often seen in athletes who have sacrificed everything to strength but have forgotten symmetry. His neck, round, not too short, but strongly made, was set so well upon his trunk that it left hardly any hollow beneath the clavicle, and the whole man gave the appearance of great strength joined to activity.

His children seeming about nineteen and twenty were not unworthy of their progenitor, and looked like copies of their father, not drawn to scale, but executed by some artist who had seen at a glance all really essential to the picture.

The band that had blared out incessantly, discoursing tangos, jazz and patriotic tunes, the chief performer, a stout negro: who on his terrific instrument, that may be best described as a mudhorn, from which no one but a member of his race seems able to extract anything but a metabolic rumbling, now ceased its fury.

A gentleman dressed in a morning coat, striped trousers, with white spats upon his patent-leather shoes, holding his tall hat in his left hand, now begged the audience to refrain from their applause during the Perestrellos' act, for he explained the slightest slip upon the wire would of necessity be fatal, for they performed without a net.

Nothing could possibly have been more pleasing to the audience, who in the way of audiences all the world over, hoped inwardly that it would be their luck to witness one of those accidents that it reads of in the Press, with so much gusto.

The girl, putting her foot into a loop, was run up lightly to the platform at one end of the wire, holding with one hand to the rope and with the other blowing kisses to the audience, as she swung through the air.

Bounding upon the platform with a skip or two, she grasped the chain supporting it and looked down upon the upturned faces, confident, youthful, and as unconscious as is a butterfly when it alights upon a flower. Her brother followed her, running up the ladder as easily as if he had been walking up a stair, his feet finding the rungs almost instinctively, as surely as in Colombia a red howling monkey passes from tree to tree. The father followed his two children, and then the girl, seizing her long white balancing pole, tripped across the wire with so much confidence that one forgot to be afraid. She turned and tripped back to the middle of the wire. Her brother joined her, and they passed one another by a miracle of equilibrium. The father, lightly as his children, ran to the centre of the ring, pretended to make a false step and fall, sat down upon the wire, rose again upon one foot, executing all his feats so easily and with such grace that the whole tent rang with applause.

Balancing a wooden chair upon the wire, the elder Perestrello seated himself upon it, looking as secure as if he had been seated in a well-padded armchair in the window of a club. His son climbed on his shoulders, sat with his legs round his father's neck, drew out a cigarette from his waistband, lighted it and smoked a puff or two, sending the smoke out in a cloud from both his nostrils, and then tossed the stump negligently into the ring. Most people would have thought that they had done enough, and put their lives in peril sufficiently to please the most avid thrill-monger. With infinite precaution, placing her feet as carefully as a steeple-jack picks his way up a tall chimney on a windy afternoon, the girl climbed like a fly upon a window-pane, so little did her feet appear to move, upon the chair, and from the back of it, on to her brother's shoulders, where she stood upright, waving a little flag. The audience held their breath, as if it were afraid to add any additional vibration to the air. Rough fishermen and peasants held their hands before their eyes, women caught tightly at the arms of those who sat beside them; the well-fed bourgeoisie were frozen in their chairs, and even those who never took their gaze off the performers had a strained look, such as you see come over sailors' faces after a close call. At last the Perestrello Family slid down the ladders to the ground. They did not skip in answer to the applause, but bowed and stood for a moment, the father's arms about the children's necks as if he recognised, that once more they were safe.

With a wild cry a troupe of Arab tumblers bounded in for the last turn. The Chinese had presented types of an old civilisation, long anterior to ours, the Perestrello Family, the poetry of the circus, but the wild-looking Arabs had a charm peculiarly their own. Probably they came from Si Hamed O'Musa in the Sus, that ancient Hollywood of Arab acrobatism that furnishes troupes of Arab tumblers to every circus in the world. Half Arab and half Berber, nothing can ever really civilise them, and though so many of them have performed in London, Paris, New York and Berlin, and speak French, German, English or what not, with perfect fluency, sometimes even marrying European wives, there are but few of them who on their holidays do not go back to the Sus, cast off their European clothes, and enjoy a sun bath of barbarism.

So lithe and active were the younger members of the troupe, so wild and flowing their great mops of hair, that it was difficult to tell which of the whirling figures, bounding and turning catherine-wheels and somersaults upon the sand, was a boy or a girl, or if there was an intermediate india-rubber sex, born in the Sus, to tumble through the world.

The elder men had the grave look that years advancing give to all Arabs, when they begin to think of Allah and interlard their speech with pious phrases. This does not take away the racial characteristic of being able to pass out of repose into the wildest ecstasies of fury. The grave and handsome elder members of the troupe, who had stood quietly whilst the boys and girls performed, occasionally encouraging them with a shrill cry, harsh as a seagull's, suddenly became animated.

Bounding across the ring, leaping and somersaulting so quickly that the eye had as much difficulty in making out their limbs as if they had been spokes of some great swift revolving wheel, they fairly outdid all the younger members of the troupe. Such leaps and such contortions, such quickness on the feet, such self-abandonment, only could be seen from those who in the zowia of Si Hamed pay homage to the saint of acrobats. With a loud cry they left the arena, some of them shaking out the sand from their long hair.

The show was over, and the audience filed out, just before midnight, as orderly and with as great decorum as if they had been coming out of church. Almost before the last of them had left the circus, workmen began to pull down everything. The dome of canvas that had appeared so permanent and as if designed to last a century, fluttered down like a gigantic moth, and men began to fold it, almost before it had ceased fluttering.

Men who but half an hour before had been models of grace and of activity, now moved about in heavy greatcoats, smoking cigarettes. Women, their hair untidy and their faces hardly streaked with the grease-paint of their make-up, flitted from caravan to caravan, or stood chattering in groups. By daybreak all was ready for the road. Nothing remained on the bare space of ground, upon the outskirts of the town, of all that microcosm of human life, its dangers, beauties, disillusions, loves, hatreds, and jealousies. Nothing was left to mark the passage of the great town of canvas that had arisen in a night, fallen in an hour and passed away, like life—nothing, except a ring upon the sand.